9.90

GHASTLY,
GHOULISH,
GRIPPING TALES

GHASTLY, GHOULISH, GRIPPING TALES

SELECTED BY
HELEN HOKE

FRANKLIN WATTS
New York / London / Toronto / Sydney
1983

A GROLIER COMPANY

Library of Congress Cataloging in Publication Data
Main entry under title:
Ghastly, ghoulish, gripping tales.

Contents: The haunted trailer / by Robert Arthur
— More spinned against / by John Wyndham —
The ski-lift / by Diana Buttenshaw — [etc.]
1. Horror tales, American. 2. Horror tales,
English. 3 Children's stories, American.
4. Children's stories, English. [1. Horror —
Fiction. 2 Short stories] I. Hoke, Helen, 1903-
PZ5.G33   [Fic]   82-17619
ISBN 0-531-04593-5

CONTENTS

OTHER ANTHOLOGIES
EDITED
BY HELEN HOKE:

Creepies, Creepies, Creepies
Fear! Fear! Fear!
Giants, Giants, Giants
Horrors, Horrors, Horrors
Jokes, Jokes, Jokes
More Ghosts, Ghosts, Ghosts
More Jokes, Jokes, Jokes
More Riddles, Riddles, Riddles
Riddles, Riddles, Riddles
Terrors, Terrors, Terrors
Weirdies, Weirdies, Weirdies

GHASTLY, GHOULISH, GRIPPING TALES

ACKNOWLEDGMENTS

The selections in this book are used by permission of and special arrangements with the proprietors of their respective copyrights, who are listed below. The editor's and publisher's thanks go to all who have made this collection possible.

The editor and publisher have made every effort to trace ownership of all material contained herein. It is their belief that the necessary permissions from publishers, authors, and authorized agents have been obtained in all cases. In the event of any questions arising as to the use of any material, the editor and publisher express regret for any error unconsciously made and will be pleased to make corrections in future editions.

"The Beetles," by Robert Bloch. © Robert Bloch 1960. Reprinted by permission of the author and the author's agents, Scott Meredith Literary Agency, Inc., 845 Third Avenue, New York/NY 10022, USA.

ABOUT THIS BOOK

Here are stories that are eerie ... monstrous ... incredible. "Terror by night"—a Biblical quotation—describes them, so perhaps you'd better read them by day or by bright lamplight— unless you positively *enjoy* being scared.

Take Diana Buttenshaw's "The Ski-Lift." Skiing has always been associated with wholesome outdoor fun. But the tale of *this* ski-lift will freeze your blood!

Here is Robert Bloch, the author of the famous *Psycho* that Alfred Hitchcock made into a movie. "The Beetles" is an appalling story that is pure horror.

Two stories provide some comic relief. They are "The Haunted Trailer," by Robert Arthur, and "More Spinned Against," by John Wyndham. In the first, some ghosts give chase. In the second, all seems fair and lovely until the shocking final paragraph.

In "His Unconquerable Enemy," by W. C. Morrow, set in India, the servant Neranya pays and pays and pays until he reverses the punishment in revenge.

In "The Horror at Chilton Castle," by Joseph Payne Brennan, a young man is willing to put an entire ocean between himself and his inheritance after seeing the contents of a hidden room.

Algernon Blackwood is an old favorite. In "A Case of Eavesdropping," a young boarder finds sleepless nights instead of peace and quiet, as numerous revelations in the next room become more real than nightmare.

"Leinigen Versus the Ants," by Carl Stephenson, is the most powerful story yet. Don't read this one if you're afraid of insects!

"The Man Who Sold Rope to the Gnoles," by Idris Seabright, is a tale of quick revenge and someone getting tangled up in spite of himself.

You're on your own: Get ready for a few (enjoyable) shocks!

Helen Hoke

THE HAUNTED TRAILER

ROBERT ARTHUR

It was inevitable, of course. Bound to happen someday. But why did it have to happen to me? What did *I do* to deserve the grief? And I was going to be married, too. I sank my last thousand dollars into that trailer, almost. In it Monica and I were going on a honeymoon tour of the United States. We were going to see the country. I was going to write, and we were going to be happy as two turtledoves.

"Ha!"

"Ha ha!"

If you detect bitterness in that laughter, I'll tell you why I'm bitter.

Because it had to be me, Mel—for Melvin—Mason who became the first person in the world to own a haunted trailer!

Now, a haunted castle is one thing. Even an ordinary haunted house can be livable in. In a castle, or a house, if there's a ghost around, you can lock yourself in the bedroom and get a little sleep. A nuisance, yes. But nothing a man couldn't put up with.

In a trailer, though! What are you going to do when you're sharing a trailer, even a super-deluxe model with four built-in bunks, a breakfast nook, a complete bathroom, a radio, electric range and easy chair, with a ghost? Where can you go to get away from it?

"Ha!"

"Ha ha!"

I've heard so much ghostly laughter the last week that I'm laughing myself that way now.

There I was. I had the trailer. I had the car to pull it, naturally. I was on my way to meet Monica in Hollywood, where she was living with an aunt from Iowa. And twelve miles west of Albany, the first night out, my brand-new, spic-and-span trailer picks up a hitchhiking haunt!

But maybe I'd better start at the beginning. It happened this way. I bought the trailer in New England—a Custom Clipper, with chrome and tan outside trim, for $2,998. I hitched it on behind my car and headed westwards, happier than a lark when the dew's on the thorn. I'd been saving up for this day for two years, and I felt wonderful.

I took it easy, getting the feel of the trailer, and so I didn't make very good time. I crossed the Hudson river just after dark, trundled through Albany in a rainstorm, and half an hour later pulled off the road into an old path between two big rocks to spend the night.

The thunder was rolling back and forth overhead, and the lightning was having target practice with the trees. But I'd picked out a nice secluded spot and I made myself comfortable. I cooked up a tasty plate of beans, some coffee, and fried potatoes. When I had eaten I took off my shoes, slumped down in the easy chair, lit a cigarette, and leaned back.

"Ah!" I said aloud. "Solid comfort. If only Monica were here, how happy we would be."

But she wasn't, so I picked up a book.

It wasn't a very good book. I must have dozed off. Maybe I slept for a couple of hours. Maybe three. Anyway, I woke with a start, the echo of a buster of a thunderbolt still rattling the willow pattern tea set in the china cupboard. My hair was standing on end from the electricity in the air.

Then the door banged open, a swirl of rain swept in, and the wind—anyway, I thought it was the wind—slammed the door to. I heard a sound like a ghost—there's no other way to describe it—of a sigh.

"Now *this*," said a voice, "is something I *like!*"

I had jumped up to shut the door, and I stood there with my unread book in my hand, gaping. The wind had blown a wisp of mist into my trailer and the mist, instead of evaporating, remained there, seeming to turn slowly and to settle into shape. It got more and more solid until—

Well, you know. It was a specter. A haunt. A homeless ghost.

The creature remained there, regarding me in a decidedly cool manner.

"Sit down, chum," it said, "and don't look so popeyed. You make me nervous. This is my first night indoors in fifteen years, and I wanta enjoy it."

"Who—" I stammered, "who—"

"I'm not," the specter retorted, "a brother owl, so don't who-who at me. What do I look like?"

"You look like a ghost," I told him.

"Now you're getting smart, chum. I *am* a ghost. What *kind* of a ghost do I look like?"

I inspected it more closely. Now that the air inside my trailer had stopped eddying, it was reasonably firm of outline.

It was a squat, heavy-set ghost, attired in ghostly garments that certainly never had come to it new. It wore the battered ghost of a felt hat, and a stubble of ghostly beard showed on his jowls.

"You look like a tramp ghost," I answered with distaste, and my uninvited visitor nodded.

"Just what I am, chum," he told me. "Call me Spike Higgins. Spike for short. That was my name before it happened."

"Before *what* happened?" I demanded. The ghost wafted across the trailer to settle down on a bunk, where he lay down and crossed his legs, hoisting one foot encased in a battered ghost of a shoe into the air.

"Before I was amachoor enough to fall asleep riding on top of a truck, and fall off right here fifteen years ago," he told me. "Ever since I been forced to haunt this place. I wasn't no Boy Scout, so I got punished by bein' made to stay here in one spot. Me, who never stayed in one spot two nights running before!

"I been gettin' kind of tired of it the last couple of years. They wouldn't even lemme haunt a house. No, I hadda do all my haunting out in th' open, where th' wind an' rain could get at me, and every dog that went by could bark at me. Chum, you don't know what it means to me that you've picked this place to stop."

"Listen," I said firmly, "you've got to get out of here!"

The apparition yawned.

"Chum," he said, "*you're* the one that's trespassin', not me. This is my happy hunting ground. Did I ask you to stop here?"

"You mean," I asked between clenched teeth, "that you won't go? You're going to stay here all night?"

"Right, chum," the ghost grunted. "Gimme a call for six a.m." He closed his eyes, and began snoring in an artificial and highly insulting manner.

Then I got sore. I threw the book at him, and it bounced off the bunk without bothering him in the least. Spike Higgins opened an eye and leered at me.

"Went right through me," he chortled. "Instead of me goin' through it. Ha ha! Ha ha ha! Joke."

"You—" I yelled, in rage. "You—stuff!"

And I slammed him with the chair cushion, which likewise went through him without doing any damage. Spike Higgins opened both eyes and stuck out his tongue at me.

Obviously I couldn't hurt him, so I got control of myself.

"Listen," I said, craftily. "You say you are doomed to haunt this spot forever? You can't leave?"

"Forbidden to leave," Spike answered. "Why?"

"Never mind," I gritted. "You'll find out."

I snatched up my raincoat and hat and scrambled out into the storm. If that ghost was doomed to remain in that spot forever, I wasn't. I got into the car, got the motor going, and backed out of there. It took a lot of maneuvering in the rain, with mud underwheel, but I made it. I got straightened out on the concrete and headed westwards.

I didn't stop until I'd covered twenty miles. Then, beginning to grin as I thought of the shock the ghost of Spike Higgins must have felt when I yanked the trailer from underneath him, I parked on a stretch of old, unused road and then crawled back into the trailer again.

Inside, I slammed the door and—

"Ha!"

"Ha ha!"

"Ha ha ha!"

Yes, more bitter laughter. Spike Higgins was still there, sound alseep and snoring.

I muttered something under my breath. Spike Higgins opened his eyes sleepily.

"Hello," he yawned. "Been having fun?"

"Listen," I finally got it out. "I—thought—you—were—doomed—to—stay—back—there—where—I—found—you—forever!"

The apparition yawned again.

"Your mistake, chum. I didn't say I was doomed to *stay*. I said I was forbidden to *leave*. I didn't leave. You hauled me away. It's all your responsibility and I'm a free agent now."

"You're a what?"

"I'm a free agent. I can ramble as far as I please. I can take up hoboing again. You've freed me. Thanks, chum. I won't forget."

"Then—then—" I sputtered. Spike Higgins nodded.

"That's right. I've adopted you. I'm going to stick with you. We'll travel together."

"But you can't!" I cried out, aghast. "Ghosts don't travel around! They haunt houses—or cemeteries—or woods. But—"

"What do you know about ghosts?" Spike Higgins' voice held sarcasm. "There's all kinds of ghosts, chum. Includin' hobo ghosts, tramp ghosts, ghosts with itchin' feet who can't stay put in one spot. Let me tell you, chum, a 'bo ghost like me ain't never had no easy time of it.

"Suppose they do give him a house to haunt? All right, he's got a roof over his head, but there he is, stuck. Houses don't move around. They don't go places. They stay in one spot till they rot.

"But things are different now. You've helped bring in a new age for the brotherhood of spooks. Now a fellow can haunt a house and be on the move at the same time. He can work at his job and still see the country. These trailers are the answer to a problem that's been bafflin' the best minds in th' spirit world for thousands of years. It's the newest thing, the latest and best. Haunted trailers. I tell you, we'll probably erect a monument to you at our next meeting. The ghost of a monument, anyway."

Spike Higgins had raised up on an elbow to make his speech. Now, grimacing, he lay back.

"That's enough, chum," he muttered. "Talking uses up my essence. I'm going to merge for a while. See you in the morning."

"Merge with what?" I asked. Spike Higgins was already so dim I could hardly see him.

"Merge with the otherwhere," a faint, distant voice told me, and Spike Higgins was gone.

I waited a minute to make sure. Then I breathed a big sigh of relief. I looked at my raincoat, at my wet feet, at the book on the floor, and knew it had all been a dream. I'd been walking in my sleep. Driving in it too. Having a nightmare.

I hung up the raincoat, slid out of my clothes and got into a bunk.

I woke up late, and for a moment felt panic. Then I breathed easily again. The other bunk was untenanted. Whistling, I jumped up, showered, dressed, ate and got under way.

It was a lovely day. Blue sky, wind, sunshine, birds singing. Thinking of Monica, I almost sang with them as I rolled down the road. In a week I'd be pulling up in front of Monica's aunt's place in Hollywood and tooting the horn—

That was the moment when a cold draught of air sighed along the back of my neck, and the short hairs rose.

I turned, almost driving into a hay wagon. Beside me was a misty figure.

"I got tired of riding back there alone," Spike Higgins told me. "I'm gonna ride up front a while an' look at th' scenery."

"You—you—" I shook with rage so that we nearly ran off

the road. Spike Higgins reached out, grabbed the wheel in tenuous fingers, and jerked us back on to our course again.

"Take it easy, chum," he said. "There's enough competition in this world I'm in, without you hornin' into th' racket."

I didn't say anything, but my thoughts must have been written on my face. I'd thought he was just a nightmare. But he was real. A ghost had moved in with me, and I hadn't the faintest idea how to move him out.

Spike Higgins grinned with a trace of malice.

"Sure, chum," he said. "It's perfectly logical. There's haunted castles, haunted palaces and haunted houses. Why not a haunted trailer?"

"Why not haunted ferryboats?" I demanded with bitterness. "Why not haunted Pullmans? Why not haunted trucks?"

"You think there ain't?" Spike Higgins' misty countenance registered surprise at my ignorance. "Could I tell you tales! There's a haunted ferryboat makes the crossing at Poughkeepsie every stormy night at midnight. There's a haunted private train on the Atchison, Santa Fe. Pal of mine haunts it. He always jumped trains, but he was a square dealer, and they gave him the private train for a reward.

"Then there's a truck on the New York Central that never gets where it's going. Never has yet. No matter where it starts out for, it winds up someplace else. Bunch of my buddies haunt it. And another truck on the Southern Pacific that never has a train to pull it. Runs by itself. It's driven I dunno how many signalmen crazy, when they saw it go past right ahead of a whole train. I could tell you—"

"Don't!" I ordered. "I forbid you to. I don't want to hear."

"Why, sure, chum," Spike Higgins agreed. "But you'll get used to it. You'll be seein' a lot of me. Because where thou ghost, I ghost. Pun." He gave a ghostly chuckle and relapsed into silence. I drove along, my mind churning. I had to get rid of him. *Had* to. Before we reached California, at the very latest. But I didn't have the faintest idea in the world how I was going to.

Then, abruptly, Spike Higgins' ghost sat up straight.

"Stop!" he ordered. "Stop, I say!"

We were on a lonely stretch of road, bordered by old cypresses, with weed-grown marshland beyond. I didn't see any reason for stopping. But Spike Higgins reached out and switched off the ignition. Then he slammed on the emergency brake. We came squealing to a stop, and just missed going into a ditch.

"What did you do that for?" I yelled. "You almost ditched us! Confound you, you ectoplasmic, hitchhiking nuisance! If I ever find a way to lay hands on you—"

"Quiet, chum!" the apparition told me rudely. "I just seen an old pal of mine. Slippery Samuels. I ain't seen him since he dropped a bottle of nitro just as he was gonna break into a bank in Mobile sixteen years ago. We're gonna give him a ride."

"We certainly are not!" I cried. "This is my car, and I'm not picking up any more—"

"It may be your car," Spike Higgins sneered, "but I'm the resident haunt, and I got full powers to extend hospitality to any buddy ghosts I want, see? Rule 11, subdivision c. Look it up. Hey, Slippery, climb in!"

A finger of fog pushed through the partly open window of the car at his hail, enlarged, and there was a second apparition on the front seat with me.

The newcomer was long and lean, just as shabbily dressed as Spike Higgins, with a ghostly countenance as mournful as a Sunday School picnic on a rainy day.

"Spike, you old son of a gun," the second spook murmured, in hollow tones that would have brought gooseflesh to a statue. "How've you been? What're you doing here? Who's *he?*"—nodding at me.

"Never mind him," Spike said disdainfully. "I'm haunting his trailer. Listen, whatever became of the old gang?"

"Still hoboing it," the long, lean apparition sighed. "Nitro Nelson is somewhere around. Pacific Pete and Buffalo Benny are lying over in a haunted jungle somewhere near Toledo. I had a date to join 'em, but a storm blew me back to Wheeling a couple of days ago."

"Mmm," Spike Higgins' ghost murmured. "Maybe we'll run into 'em. Let's go back in my trailer and do a little chinning. As for you, chum, make camp any time you want. Ta ta."

The two apparitions oozed through the back of the car and were gone. I was boiling inside, but there was nothing I could do.

I drove on for another hour, went through Toledo, then stopped at a wayside camp. I paid my dollar, picked out a spot and parked.

But when I entered the trailer, the ghosts of Spike Higgins and Slippery Samuels, the bank robber, weren't there. Nor had they shown up by the time I finished dinner. In fact I ate, washed and got into bed with no sign of them.

Breathing a prayer that maybe Higgins had abandoned me to go back to 'boing it in the spirit world, I feel asleep. And began to dream. About Monica—

When I woke, there was a sickly smell in the air, and the heavy staleness of old tobacco smoke.

I opened my eyes. Luckily, I opened them prepared for the worst. Even so, I wasn't prepared well enough.

Spike Higgins was back. Ha! Ha ha! Ha ha ha! I'll say he was back. He lay on the opposite bunk, his eyes shut, his mouth open, snoring. Just the ghost of a snore, but quite loud enough. On the bunk above him lay his bank-robber companion. In the easy chair was slumped a third apparition, short and stout, with a round, whiskered face. A tramp spirit, too.

So was the ghost stretched out on the floor, gaunt and cadaverous. So was the small, mournful spook in the bunk above me, his ectoplasmic hand swinging over the side, almost in my face. Tramps, all of them. Hobo spooks. Five hobo phantoms asleep in my trailer!

And there were cigarette butts in all the ash-trays, and burns on my built-in writing desk. The cigarettes apparently had just been lit and let burn. The air was choking with stale smoke, and I had a headache I could have sold for a fire alarm, it was ringing so loudly in my skull.

I knew what had happened. During the night Spike Higgins and his pal had rounded up some more of their ex-hobo companions. Brought them back. To *my* trailer. Now—I was so angry I saw all five of them through a red haze that gave their ectoplasm a ruby tinge. Then I got hold of myself. I couldn't throw them out. I couldn't harm them. I couldn't touch them.

No, there was only one thing I could do. Admit I was beaten. Take my loss and quit while I could. It was a bitter pill to swallow. But if I wanted to reach Monica, if I wanted to enjoy the honeymoon we'd planned, I'd have to give up the fight.

I got into my clothes. Quietly I sneaked out, locking the trailer behind me. Then I hunted for the owner of the trailer camp, a lanky man, hard-eyed, but well dressed. I guessed he must have money.

"Had sort of a party last night, hey?" he asked me, with a leering wink. "I seen lights, an' heard singing, long after midnight. Not loud, though, so I didn't bother you. But it looked like somebody was havin' a high old time."

I gritted my teeth.

"That was me," I said, "I couldn't sleep. I got up and turned on the radio. Truth is, I haven't slept a single night in that trailer. I guess I wasn't built for trailer life. That job cost me $2,998 new, just three days ago. I've got the bill of sale. How'd you like to buy it for fifteen hundred, and make two hundred easy profit on it?"

He gnawed his lip, but knew the trailer was a bargain. We settled for thirteen-fifty. I gave him the bill of sale, took the money, uncoupled, got into the car and left there.

As I turned the bend in the road, heading westwards, there was no sign that Spike Higgins' ghost was aware of what had happened.

I even managed to grin as I thought of his rage when he woke up to find I had abandoned him. It was almost worth the money I'd lost to think of it.

Beginning to feel better, I stepped on the accelerator, piling up miles between me and that trailer. At least I was rid of Spike Higgins and his friends.

"Ha!"

"Ha ha!"

"Ha ha ha!"

That's what I thought.

About the middle of the afternoon I was well into Illinois. It was open country, and monotonous, so I turned on my radio. And the first thing I got was a police broadcast.

"All police, Indiana and Illinois! Be on the watch for a tan-and-chrome trailer, stolen about noon from a camp near Toledo. The thieves are believed heading west in it. That is all."

I gulped. It couldn't be! But—it sounded like my trailer,

all right. I looked in my rear-vision mirror, apprehensively. The road behind was empty. I breathed a small sigh of relief. I breathed it too soon. For at that moment, round a curve half a mile behind me, something swung into sight and came racing down the road after me.

The trailer.

"Ha!"

"Ha ha!"

There it came, a tan streak that zipped around the curve and came streaking after me, zigzagging wildly from side to side of the road, doing at least sixty—without a car pulling it.

My flesh crawled, and my hair stood on end. I stepped on the accelerator. Hard. And I picked up speed in a hurry. In half a minute I was doing seventy, and the trailer was still gaining. Then I hit eighty—and passed a motorcycle cop parked beside the road.

I had just a glimpse of his popeyed astonishment as I whizzed past, with the trailer chasing me fifty yards behind. Then, kicking on his starter, he slammed after us.

Meanwhile, in spite of everything the car would do, the trailer pulled up behind me and I heard the coupling clank as it was hitched on. At once my speed dropped. The trailer was swerving dangerously, and I had to slow. Behind me the cop was coming, siren open wide, but I didn't worry about him because Spike Higgins was materializing beside me.

"Whew!" he said, grinning at me. "My essence feels all used up. Thought you could give Spike Higgins and his pals the slip, huh? You'll learn, chum, you'll learn. That trooper looks like a tough baby. You'll have fun trying to talk yourself out of this."

"Yes, but see what it'll get *you,* you ectoplasmic excrescence!" I raged at him. "The trailer will be stored away in some

county garage for months as evidence while I'm being held for
trial on the charge of stealing it. And how'll you like haunting a
garage?"

Higgins' face changed.

"Say, that's right," he muttered. "My first trip for fifteen
years, too."

He put his fingers to his lips, and blew the shrill ghost of a
whistle. In a moment the car was filled with cold, clammy
draughts as Slippery Samuels and the other three apparitions
appeared in the seat beside Higgins.

Twisting and turning and seeming to intermingle a lot,
they peered out at the cop, who was beside the car now, one
hand on his gun butt, trying to crowd me over to the shoulder.

"All right, boys!" Higgins finished explaining. "You know
what we gotta do. Me an' Slippery'll take the car. You guys
take the trailer."

They slipped through the open windows like smoke. Then
I saw Slippery Samuels holding on to the left front bumper,
and Spike Higgins holding on to the right, their ectoplasm
streaming out horizontal to the road, stretched and thinned by
the air rush. And an instant later we began to move with a
speed I had never dreamed of reaching.

We zipped ahead of the astonished cop, and the speedometer needle began to climb again. It took the trooper an
instant to believe his eyes. Then with a yell he yanked out his
gun and fired. A bullet bumbled past; then he was too busy
trying to overtake us again to shoot.

The speedometer said ninety now, and was still climbing.
It touched a hundred and stuck there. I was trying to pray when
down the road a mile away I saw a sharp curve, a bridge and a
deep river. I froze. I couldn't even yell.

We came up to the curve so fast that I was still trying to

move my lips when we hit it. I didn't make any effort to take it. Instead I slammed on the brakes and prepared to plough straight ahead into a fence, a stand of young poplars and the river.

But just as I braked, I heard Spike Higgins' ghostly scream, "Allay-OOP!"

And before we reached the ditch, car and trailer swooped up in the air. An instant later at a height of a hundred and fifty feet, we hurtled straight westwards over the river and the town beyond.

I'd like to have seen the expression on the face of the motorcycle cop then. As far as that goes, I'd like to have seen my own.

Then the river was behind us, and the town, and we were swooping down towards a dank, gloomy-looking patch of woods through which ran an abandoned railway line. A moment later we struck earth with a jouncing shock and came to rest.

Spike Higgins and Slippery Samuels let go of the bumpers and straightened themselves up. Spike Higgins dusted ghostly dust off his palms and leered at me.

"How was that, chum?" he asked. "Neat, hey?"

"How—" I stuttered, "how—"

"Simple," Spike Higgins answered. "Anybody that can tip tables can do it. Just levitation, 'at's all. Hey, meet the boys. You ain't been introduced yet. This is Buffalo Benny, this one is Toledo Ike, this one Pacific Pete."

The fat spook, the cadaverous one, and the melancholy little one appeared from behind the car, and smirked as Higgins introduced them. Then Higgins waved a hand impatiently.

"C'm on, chum," he said. "There's a road there that takes

us out of these woods. Let's get going. It's almost dark, and we
don't wanna spend the night here. This used to be in Dan
Bracer's territory."

"Who's Dan Bracer?" I demanded, getting the motor
going, because I was as anxious to get away from there as Spike
Higgins' spook seemed to be.

"Just a railway dick," Spike Higgins, said, with a distinctly
uneasy grin. "Toughest bull that ever kicked a poor 'bo off a
freight."

"So mean he always drank black coffee," Slippery
Samuels put in, in a mournful voice. "Cream turned sour when
he picked up the jug."

"Not that we was afraid of him—" Buffalo Benny, the fat
apparition, squeaked. "But—"

"We just never liked him," Toledo Ike croaked, a sickly
look on his ghostly features. "O' course, he ain't active now. He
was retired a couple years back, an' jes' lately I got a rumor he
was sick."

"Dyin'," Pacific Peter murmured hollowly.

"Dyin'." They all sighed the word, looking apprehensive.
Then Spike Higgins' ghost scowled truculently at me.

"Never mind about Dan Bracer," he snapped. "Let's just
get goin' out of here. And don't give that cop no more thought.
You think a cop is gonna turn in a report that a car and trailer
he was chasin' suddenly sailed up in the air an' flew away like an
aeroplane? Not on your sweet life. He ain't gonna say nothing
to nobody about it."

Apparently he was right, because after I had driven out of
the woods, with some difficulty, and onto the secondary
highway, there was no further sign of pursuit. I headed
westwards again, and Spike Higgins and his pals moved back
to the trailer, where they lolled about, letting my cigarettes

burn and threatening to call the attention of the police to me when I complained.

I grew steadily more morose and desperate as the Pacific Coast, and Monica, came nearer. I was behind schedule, due to Spike Higgins' insistence on my taking a roundabout route so they could see the Grand Canyon, and no way to rid myself of the obnoxious haunts appeared. I couldn't even abandon the trailer. Spike Higgins had been definite on that point. It was better to haul a haunted trailer around than to have one chasing you, he pointed out, and shuddering at the thought of being pursued by a trailer full of ghosts wherever I went, I agreed.

But if I couldn't get rid of them, it meant no Monica, no marriage, no honeymoon. And I was determined that nothing as insubstantial as a spirit was going to interfere with my life's happiness.

Just the same, by the time I had driven over the mountains and into California, I was almost on the point of doing something desperate. Apparently sensing this, Spike Higgins and the others had been on their good behavior. But I could still see no way to get rid of them.

It was early afternoon when I finally rolled into Hollywood, haggard and unshaven, and found a trailer camp, where I parked. Heavy-hearted, I bathed and shaved and put on clean clothes. I didn't know what I was going to say to Monica, but I was already several days behind schedule, and I couldn't put off ringing her.

There was a telephone in the camp office. I looked up Ida Bracer—her aunt's name—in the book, then put through the call.

Monica herself answered. Her voice sounded distraught.

"Oh, Mel," she exclaimed, as soon as I announced myself, "where have you been? I've been expecting you for days."

"I was delayed," I told her, bitterly. "Spirits. I'll explain later."

"Spirits?" Her tone seemed cold. "Well, anyway, now that you're here at last, I must see you at once. Mel, Uncle Dan is dying."

"Uncle Dan?" I echoed.

"Yes, Aunt Ida's brother. He used to live in Iowa, but a few months ago he was taken ill, and he came out to be with Aunt and me. Now he's dying. The doctor says it's only a matter of hours."

"Dying?" I repeated again. "Your Uncle Dan, from Iowa, dying?"

Then it came to me. I began to laugh. Exultantly.

"I'll be right over!" I said, and hung up.

Still chuckling, I hurried out and unhitched my car. Spike Higgins stared at me suspiciously.

"Just got an errand to do," I said airily. "Be back soon."

"You better be," Spike Higgins' ghost said. "We wanta drive around and see those movie stars' houses later on."

Ten minutes later Monica herself, trim and lovely, was opening the door for me. In high spirits, I grabbed her around the waist, and kissed her. She turned her cheek to me, then, releasing herself, looked at me strangely.

"Mel," she frowned, "what in the world is wrong with you?"

"Nothing," I carolled. "Monica darling, I've got to talk to your uncle."

"But he's too sick to see anyone. He's sinking fast, the doctor says."

"All the more reason why I must see him," I told her, and pushed into the house. "Where is he, upstairs?"

I hurried up, and into the sickroom. Monica's uncle, a big man with a rugged face and a chin like the prow of a battleship, was in bed, breathing stertorously.

"Mr. Bracer!" I said, breathless, and his eyes opened slowly.

"Who're you?" a voice as raspy as a shovel scraping a concrete floor growled.

"I'm going to marry Monica," I told him. "Mr. Bracer, have you ever heard of Spike Higgins? Or Slippery Samuels? Or Buffalo Benny, Pacific Peter, Toledo Ike?"

"*Heard* of 'em?" A bright glow came into the sick man's eyes. "Ha! I'll say I have. And laid hands on 'em, too, more'n once. But they're dead now."

"I know they are," I told him. "But they're still around. Mr. Bracer, how'd you like to meet up with them again?"

"Would I!" Dan Bracer murmured, and his hands clenched in unconscious anticipation. "Ha!"

"Then," I said, "if you'll wait for me in the cemetery the first night after—after—well, anyway, wait for me, and I'll put you in touch with them."

The ex-railway detective nodded. He grinned broadly, like a tiger viewing its prey, and eager to be after it. Then he lay back, his eyes closed, and Monica, running in, gave a little gasp.

"He's gone!" she said.

"Ha ha!" I chuckled. "Ha ha ha! What a surprise this is going to be to certain parties."

The funeral was held in the afternoon, two days later. I didn't see Monica much in the interim. In the first place, though she hadn't known her uncle well, and wasn't particularly grieved, there were a lot of details to be attended to. In the second place, Spike Higgins and his pals kept me on the jump. I had to drive around Hollywood, to all the stars' houses, to Malibu Beach,

Santa Monica, Laurel Canyon and the various studios, so they could sightsee.

Then, too, Monica rather seemed to be avoiding me, when I did have time free. But I was too inwardly gleeful at the prospect of getting rid of the ghosts of Higgins and his pals to notice.

I managed to slip away from Higgins to attend the funeral of Dan Bracer, but could not help grinning broadly, and even at times chuckling, as I thought of his happy anticipation of meeting Spike Higgins and the others again. Monica eyed me oddly, but I could explain later. It wasn't quite the right moment to go into details.

After the funeral, Monica said she had a headache, so I promised to come around later in the evening. I returned to the trailer to find Spike Higgins and the others sprawled out, smoking my cigarettes again. Higgins looked at me with dark suspicion.

"Chum," he said, "we wanta be hitting the road again. We leave tomorrow, get me?"

"Tonight, Spike," I said cheerfully. "Why wait? Right after sunset you'll be on your way. To distant parts. Tra la, tra le, tum tum te tum."

He scowled, but could think of no objection. I waited impatiently for sunset. As soon as it was thoroughly dark, I hitched up and drove out of the trailer camp, heading for the cemetery where Dan Bracer had been buried that afternoon.

Spike Higgins was still surly, but unsuspicious until I drew up and parked by the low stone wall at the nearest point to Monica's uncle's grave. Then, gazing out at the darkness-shadowed cemetery, he looked uneasy.

"Say." he snarled, "watcha stoppin' here for? Come on, let's be movin'."

"In a minute, Spike," I said. "I have some business here."
I slid out and hopped over the low rail.

"Mr. Bracer!" I called. "Mr. Bracer!"

I listened, but a long freight rumbling by half a block distant, where the Union Pacific lines entered the city, drowned out any sound. For a moment I could see nothing. Then a misty figure came into view among the headstones.

"Mr. Bracer!" I called as it approached. "This way!"

The figure headed towards me. Behind me Spike Higgins, Slippery Samuels and the rest of the ghostly crew were pressed against the wall, staring apprehensively into the darkness, and they were able to recognize the dim figure approaching before I could be sure of it.

"Dan Bracer!" Spike Higgins choked, in a high, ghostly squeal.

"It's him!" Slippery Samuels groaned.

"In the spirit!" Pacific Pete wailed. "Oh oh oh oh OH!"

They tumbled backwards, with shrill squeaks of dismay. Dan Bracer's spirit came forward faster. Paying no attention to me, he took off after the retreating five.

Higgins turned and fled, wildly, with the others at his heels. They were heading towards the railway line, over which the freight was still rumbling, and Dan Bracer was now at their heels.

Crowding each other, Higgins and Slippery Samuels and Buffalo Benny swung onto a passing truck, with Pacific Pete and Toledo Ike catching wildly at the rungs of the next.

They drew themselves up to the top of the trucks, and stared back. Dan Bracer's ghost seemed, for an instant, about to be left behind. But one long ectoplasmic arm shot out. A ghostly hand caught the rail of the guard's van, and Dan Bracer swung aboard. A moment later, he was running forward along the tops of the trucks, and up ahead of him, Spike Higgins and his pals were racing towards the engine.

That was the last I saw of them—five phantom figures fleeing, the sixth pursuing in happy anticipation. Then they were gone out of my life, heading east.

Still laughing to myself at the manner in which I had rid myself of Spike Higgins' ghost, and so made it possible for Monica and me to be married and enjoy our honeymoon trailer trip after all, I drove to Monica's aunt's house.

"Melvin!" Monica said sharply, as she answered my ring. "What are you laughing about now?"

"Your uncle," I chuckled. "He—"

"My uncle! Monica gasped. "You—you fiend! You laughed when he died! You laughed all during his funeral! Now you're laughing because he's dead!"

"No, Monica!" I said. "Let me explain. About the spirits, and how I—"

Her voice broke.

"Forcing your way into the house—laughing at my poor Uncle Dan—laughing at his funeral—"

"But Monica!" I cried. "It isn't that way at all. I've just been to the cemetery, and—"

"And you came back laughing," Monica retorted. "I never want to see you again. Our engagement is broken. And worst of all is the *way* you laugh. It's so—so ghostly! So spooky. Blood-chilling. Even if you hadn't done the other things, I could never marry a man who laughs like that. So here's your ring. And good-bye."

Leaving me staring at the ring in my hand, she slammed the door. And that was that. Monica is very strong-minded, and what she says, she means. I couldn't even try to explain. About Spike Higgins. And how I'd unconsciously come to laugh that way through associating with five phantoms. After all, I'd just rid myself of them for good. And the only way Monica would ever have believed my story would have been from my showing her Spike Higgins' ghost himself.

"Ha!"

"Ha ha!"

"Ha ha ha ha!"

If you know anyone who wants to buy a practically unused trailer, cheap, let them get in touch with me.

MORE SPINNED AGAINST

JOHN WYNDHAM

One of the things about her husband that displeased Lydia Charters more as the years went by was the shape of him: another was his hobby. There were other displeasures, of course, but it was these in particular that rankled her with a sense of failure.

True, he had been much the same shape when she had married him, but she had looked for improvement. She had envisioned the development, under her domestic influence, of a more handsome, suaver, better-filled type. Yet, after nearly twelve years of her care and feeding there was scarcely any demonstrable improvement. The torso, the main man, looked a little more solid, and the scales endorsed that it was so, but, unfortunately, this simply seemed to have the result of emphasizing the knobby, gangling, loosely hinged effect of the rest.

Once, in a mood of more than usual dissatisfaction, Lydia had taken a pair of his trousers, and measured them carefully. Inert, and empty, they seemed all right—long in the leg, naturally, but not abnormally so, and the usual width that people wore—but, put to use, they immediately achieved the effect of being too narrow and full of knobs, just as his sleeves did. After the failure of several ideas to soften this appearance, she had realized that she would have to put up with it. Reluctantly, she had told herself: "Well, I suppose it can't be helped. It must be just one of those things—like horsy women getting to look more like horses, I mean," and thereby managed to dig at the hobby, as well.

Hobbies are convenient in the child, but irritating in the adult; which is why women are careful never to have them, but simply to be "interested" in this or that. It is perfectly natural for a woman—and Lydia was a comely demonstration of the art of being one—to take an interest in semi-precious—and when she can afford them—precious stones: Edward's hobby, on the other hand, was not really natural to anyone.

Lydia had known about the hobby before they were married, of course. No one could know Edward for long without being aware of the way his eyes hopefully roved the corners of any room he chanced to be in, or how, when he was out of doors, his attention would be suddenly snatched away from any matter in hand by the sight of a pile of dead leaves, or a piece of loose bark. It had been irritating at times, but she had not allowed it to weigh too much with her, since it would naturally wither from neglect later. For Lydia held the not uncommon opinion that though, of course, a married man should spend a certain amount of his time assuring an income, beyond that there ought to be only one interest in life—from which it followed that the existence of any other must be slightly insulting to his wife, since everybody knows that a hobby is really just a form of sublimation.

The withering, however, had not taken place.

Disappointing as this was in itself, it would have been a lot more tolerable if Edward's hobby had been the collection of objects of standing—say, old prints, or first editions, or oriental poetry. That kind of thing could not only be displayed for envy, it had value; and the collector himself had status. But no one achieved the status of being more than a crank for having even a very extensive collection of spiders.

Even over butterflies or moths, Lydia felt without actually putting the matter to the test, one could perhaps have summoned up the appearance of some enthusiasm. There was a kind of nature's-living-jewel's line that one could take if they were nicely mounted. But for spiders—a lot of nasty, creepy-crawly, leggy horrors, all getting gradually more pallid in tubes of alcohol—she could find nothing to be said at all.

In the early days of their marriage, Edward had tried to give her some of his own enthusiasm, and Lydia had listened as tactfully as possible to his explanation of the complicated lives, customs, and mating-habits of spiders, most of which seemed either disgusting, or very short on morals, or frequently both, and to his expectations on the beauties of coloration and marking which her eye lacked the affection to detect. Luckily, however, it had gradually become apparent from some of her comments and questions that Edward was not awakening the sympathetic understanding he had hoped for, and when the attempt lapsed Lydia had been able to retreat gratefully to her former viewpoint from which all spiders were undesirable, and the dead only slightly less horrible than the living.

Realizing that frontal opposition to spiders would be poor

tactics, she had attempted a quiet and painless weaning. It had taken her two or three years to appreciate that this was not going to work; after that, the spiders had settled down to being one of those bits of the rough that the wise take with the smooth and leave unmentioned except on those occasions of extreme provocation when the whole catalogue of one's dissatisfactions is reviewed.

Lydia entered Edward's spider-room about once a week, partly to tidy and dust it, and partly to enjoy detesting its inhabitants in a pleasantly masochistic fashion. This she could do on at least two levels. There was the kind of generalized satisfaction that anyone might feel in looking along the rows of test tubes that, at any rate, here were a whole lot of displeasing creepies that would creep no more. And then there was the more personal sense of compensation in the reflection that though they had to some extent succeeded in diverting a married man's attention from its only proper target, they had to die to do it.

There was an astonishing number of test tubes ranged in the racks along the walls, so many that at one time she had hopefully inquired whether there could be many more kinds of spiders. His first answer of five hundred and sixty in the British Isles had been quite encouraging, but then he had gone on to speak of twenty thousand or so different kinds in the world, not to mention the allied orders, whatever they might be, in a way that was depressing.

There were other things in the room beside the test tubes; a shelf of reference books, a card-index, a table holding his carefully hooded microscope. There was also a long bench against one wall supporting a variety of bottles, packets of slides, boxes of new test tubes, as well as a number of glass-topped boxes in which specimens were preserved for study alive before they went into alcohol.

Lydia could never resist peeping into these condemned cells with a satisfaction which she would scarcely have cared to admit, or, indeed, even have felt in the case of other creatures, but somehow with spiders it just served them right for being spiders. As a rule there would be five or six of them in similar boxes, and it was with surprise one morning that she noticed a large bell jar ranged neatly in the line. After she had done the rest of the dusting, curiosity took her over to the bench. It could of course, have been much easier to observe the occupant of the bell jar than those of the boxes, but in fact it was not because the inside, for fully two-thirds of its heights, was obscured by web. A web so thickly woven as to hide the occupant entirely from the sides. It hung in folds, almost like a drapery, and on examining it more closely, Lydia was impressed by the ingenuity of the work; it looked surprisingly like a set of Nottingham lace curtains—though greatly reduced in scale, of course, and perhaps not quite in the top flight of design. Lydia went closer to look over the top edge of the web, and down upon the occupant. "Good gracious!" she said.

The spider squatting in the center of its web-screened circle was quite the largest she had ever seen. She stared at it. She recalled that Edward had been in a state of some excitement the previous evening, but she had paid little attention except to tell him, as on several previous occasions, that she was much too busy to go and look at a horrible spider; she also recalled that he had been somewhat hurt about her lack of interest. Now, seeing the spider, she could understand that: she could even understand for once how it was possible to talk of a beautifully colored spider, for there could be no doubt at all that this specimen deserved a place in the nature's-living-jewels class. The ground color was a pale green with a darker stippling, which faded away toward the underside. Down the center of the back ran a pattern of blue arrowheads, bright in the center and merging almost into the green at the points. Touches of the same scarlet showed at the joints of the green legs, and there were small markings of it, too, on the upper part of what Edward resoundingly called the cephalothorax, but which Lydia thought of as the part where the legs were fastened on.

Lydia leaned closer. Strangely, the spider had not frozen into immobility in the usual spiderish manner. Its attention seemed to be wholly taken up by something held out between its front pair of legs, something that flashed as it moved. Lydia thought that the object was an aquamarine, cut and polished. As she moved her head to make sure, her shadow fell across the bell jar. The spider stopped twiddling the stone, and froze. Presently, a small, muffled voice said:

"Hello! Who are you?" with a slight foreign accent.

Lydia looked around. The room was as empty as before.

"No. Here!" said the muffled voice.

She looked down again at the jar, and saw the spider pointing to itself with its number two leg on the right.

"My name," said the voice, sociably, "is Arachne. What's yours?"

"Er—Lydia," said Lydia uncertainly.

"Oh, dear! Why?" asked the voice.

Lydia felt a trifle nettled. "What do you mean, why?" she asked.

"Well, as I recall it, Lydia was sent to hell as a punishment for doing very nasty things to her lover. I suppose you aren't given to—?"

"Certainly not," Lydia said, cutting her voice short.

"Oh," said the voice doubtfully. "Still, they can't have given you the name for nothing. And mind you, I never really blamed Lydia. Lovers, in my experience, usually deserve—" Lydia lost the rest as she looked around the room uncertainly.

"I don't understand," she said. "I mean, is it really—?"

"Oh, it's me, all right," said the spider. And to make sure, it indicated itself again, this time with the third leg on the left.

"But—but spiders can't—"

"Of course not. Not *real* spiders, but I'm Arachne—I told you that."

A hazy memory stirred at the back of Lydia's mind.

"You mean *the* Arachne?" she inquired.

"Did you ever hear of another?" the voice asked coldly.

"I mean, the one who annoyed Athene—though I can't remember just how?" said Lydia.

"Certainly. I was technically a spinster, and Athene was jealous and—"

"I should have thought it would be the other way—oh, I see, you mean you spun?"

"That's what I said. I was the best spinner and weaver, and when I won the all-Greece open competition and beat Athene she couldn't take it; she was furiously jealous and so she turned me into a spider. It's very unfair to let gods and goddesses go in for competitions at all, I always say. They're spitefully bad losers, and then they go telling lies about you to justify the bad-tempered things they do in revenge. You've probably heard it differently?" the voice added, challenging slightly.

"No, I think it was pretty much like that," Lydia told her, tactfully. "You must have been a spider a very long time now," she added.

"Yes, I suppose so, but you give up counting after a bit." The voice paused, then it went on: "I say, would you mind taking this glass thing off? It's stuffy in here; besides I shouldn't have to shout."

Lydia hesitated.

"I never interfere with anything in this room. My husband gets so annoyed if I do."

"Oh, you needn't be afraid I shall run away. I'll give you my word on that, if you like."

But Lydia was still doubtful.

"You're in a pretty desperate position, you know," she said, with an involuntary glance at the alcohol bottle.

"Not really," said the voice in a tone that suggested a shrug. "I've often been caught before. Something always turns up—it *has* to. That's one of the few advantages of having a real permanent curse on you. It makes it impossible for anything really fatal to happen."

Lydia looked around. The window was shut, the door, too, and the fireplace was blocked up.

"Well, perhaps for a few minutes, if you promise," she allowed.

She lifted the jar and put it down to one side. As she did so the curtains of web trailed out, and tore.

"Never mind about them. Phew! That's better," said the voice, still small, but now quite clear and distinct.

The spider did not move. It still held the aquamarine, catching the light and shining, between its front legs.

On a sudden thought, Lydia leaned down and looked at the stone more closely. She was relieved to see that it was not one of her own.

"Pretty, isn't it?" said Arachne. "Not really my color, though. I rather kill it, I think. One of the emeralds would have been more suitable—even though they were smaller."

"Where did you get it?" Lydia asked.

"Oh, a house just near here. Next door but one, I think it was."

"Mrs. Ferris's—yes, of course, that would be one of hers."

"Possibly," agreed Arachne. "Anyway, it was in a cabinet with a lot of others, so I took it, and I was just coming through the hedge out of the garden, looking for a comfortable hole to enjoy it, when I got caught. It was the stone shining that made him see me. A funny sort of man, rather like a spider himself, if he had had more legs."

Lydia said, somewhat coldly: "He was smarter than you were."

"H'm," said Arachne, noncommittally.

She laid the stone down, and started to move about, trailing several threads from her spinnerets. Lydia drew away a little. For a moment she watched Arachne, who appeared to be engaged in a kind of doodling, then her eyes returned to the aquamarine.

"I have a little collection of stones myself. Not as good as Mrs. Ferris's, of course, but one or two nice ones amongst them," she remarked.

"Oh," said Arachne, absentminded as she worked out her pattern.

"I—I should rather like a nice aquamarine," said Lydia. "Suppose the door happened to have been left open just a little..."

"There," said Arachne, with satisfaction. "Isn't that the prettiest doiley you ever saw?"

She paused to admire her work.

Lydia looked at it, too. The pattern seemed to her to show a lack of subtlety, but she agreed tactfully. "It's delightful! Absolutely charming! I wish I could—I mean, I don't know how you do it."

"One has just a little talent, you know," said Archne, with undeceiving modesty. "You were saying something?" she added.

Lydia repeated her remark.

"Not really worth my while," said Arachne. "I told you something *has* to happen, so why should I bother?"

She began to doodle again. Rapidly, though with a

slightly abstracted air, she constructed another small lace mat suitable for the lower-income-bracket trade, and pondered over it for a moment. Presently she said:

"Of course, if it were to be *made* worth my while . . ."

"I couldn't afford very much—" began Lydia, with caution.

"Not money," said Arachne. "What on earth would I do with money? But I am a bit overdue for a holiday."

"Holiday?" Lydia repeated, blankly.

"There's a sort of alleviation clause," Arachne explained. "Lots of good curses have them. It's often something like being uncursed by a prince's kiss—you know, something so improbable that it's a real outside chance, but gets the god a reputation for not being such a Shylock after all. Mine is that I'm allowed twenty-four hours holiday in the year—but I've scarcely ever had it."

She paused, doodling an inch or two of lace edging.

"You see," she added, "the difficult thing is to find someone willing to change places for twenty-four hours."

"Er—yes, I can see it would be," said Lydia detachedly.

Arachne put out one foreleg and spun the aquamarine around so that it glittered.

"Someone willing to change places," she repeated.

"Well—er—I—er—I don't think—" Lydia tried.

"It's not at all difficult to get in and out of Mrs. Ferris's house—not when you're my size," Arachne observed.

Lydia looked at the aquamarine. It wasn't possible to stop having a mental picture of the other stones that were lying bedded on black velvet in Mrs. Ferris's cabinet.

"Suppose one got caught?" she suggested.

"One need not bother about that—except as an inconvenience. I should have to take over in twenty-four hours again, in any case," Arachne told her.

"Well—I don't know—" said Lydia, unwillingly.

Arachne spoke in a ruminative manner:

"I remember thinking how easy it would be to carry them out one by one, and hide them in a convenient hole," she said.

Lydia was never able later to recall in detail the succeeding stages of the conversation, only that at some point where she was still intending to be tentative and hypothetical, Arachne must have thought she was more definite. Anyway, one moment she was standing beside the bench, and the next, it seems, she was on it, and the thing had happened.

She didn't really feel any different, either. Six eyes did not seem any more difficult to manage than two, though everything looked exceedingly large and the opposite wall very far away. The eight legs seemed capable of managing themselves without getting tangled, too.

"How do you? Oh, I see," she said.

"Steady on," said a voice from above. "That's more than enough for a pair of curtains you've wasted there. Take it gently, now. Always keep the word 'dainty' in mind. Yes, that's much better—a little finer still. That's it. You'll soon get the idea. Now all you have to do is walk over the edge, and let yourself down on it."

"Er—yes," said Lydia dubiously. The edge of the bench seemed a long way from the floor.

"Oh, there's just one thing," she said. "About men?"

"Men?" said Lydia.

"Well, male spiders, I mean. I don't want to come back and find that—"

"No, of course not," agreed Lydia. "I shall be pretty busy, I expect. And I don't—er—think I feel much interested in male spiders, as a matter of fact."

"Well, I don't know. It's a matter of like calling to like."

"I think it sort of probably depends on how long you have been like," suggested Lydia.

"Good. Anyway, it's not very difficult. He'll only be about a sixteenth of your size, so you can easily brush him off. Or you can eat him, if you like."

"*Eat* him!" exclaimed Lydia. "Oh, yes, I remember my husband said something—No, I think I'll just brush him off, as you said."

"Just as you like. There's one thing about spiders, they're much better arranged to the female advantage. You don't have to go on being cumbered up with a useless male just because. You simply find a new one when you want him. It simplifies things a lot, really."

"I suppose so," said Lydia. "Still, only twenty-four hours—"

"Quite," said Arachne. "Well, I'll be off. I mustn't waste my holiday. You'll find you'll be quite all right once you get the hang of it. Good-bye till tomorrow." And she went out, leaving the door slightly ajar.

Lydia practiced her spinning a little more until she could be sure of keeping a fairly even thread. Then she went to the edge of the bench. After a slight hesitation she let herself over. It turned out to be quite easy, really.

Indeed, the whole thing turned out to be far easier than she had expected. She found her way to Mrs. Ferris's drawing room, where the door of the cabinet had been carelessly left unlatched, and selected a nice fire opal. There was no difficulty in discovering a small hole on the roadside of the front bank in which the booty could be deposited for collection later. On the next trip she chose a small ruby; and the next time an excellently cut square zircon, and the operation settled down to an industrious routine which was interrupted by nothing more than the advance of a couple of male spiders who were easily

bowled over with a flip of the front leg, and became dis-
couraged.

By the late afternoon Lydia had accumulated quite a nice
little hoard in the hole in the bank. She was in the act of adding
a small topaz, and wondering whether she would make just one
more trip, when a shadow fell across her. She froze quite still,
looking up at a tall gangling form with knobby joints, which
really did look surprisingly spidery from that angle.

"Well, I'm damned," said Edward's voice, speaking to
itself. "Another one! Two in two days. Extraordinary."

Then, before Lydia could make up her mind what to do, a
sudden darkness descended over her, and presently she found
herself being joggled along in a box.

A few minutes later she was under the bell jar that she had
lifted off Arachne, with Edward bending over her, looking
partly annoyed at finding his specimen had escaped, and partly
elated that he had recaptured it.

After that, there didn't seem to be much to do but doodle a
few lace curtains for privacy, in the way Arachne had. It was a
consoling thought that the stones were safely cached away, and
that any time after the next twelve or thirteen hours, she would
be able to collect them at her leisure...."

No one came near the spider-room during the evening. Lydia
could distinguish various domestic sounds taking place in
more or less their usual succession, and culminating in two
pairs of footfalls ascending the stairs. And but for physical
handicaps, she might have frowned slightly at this point. The
ethics of the situation were somewhat obscure. Was Arachne
really entitled...? Oh, well, there was nothing one could do
about it, anyway....

Presently the sound of movement ceased, and the house
settled down for the night.

She had half-expected that Edward would look in to assure himself of her safety before he went to work in the morning. She remembered that he had done so in the case of other and far less spectacular spiders, and she was a trifle piqued that when at last the door did open, it was simply to admit Arachne. She noticed, also, that Arachne had not succeeded in doing her hair with just that touch that suited Lydia's face.

Arachne gave a little yawn, and came across to the bench.

"Hullo," she said, lifting the jar, "had an interesting time?"

"Not *this* part of it," Lydia said. "Yesterday was very satisfactory, though. I hope you enjoyed your holiday."

"Yes," said Arachne. "Yes, I had a nice time—though it did somehow seem less of a change than I'd hoped." She looked at the watch on her wrist. "Well, time's nearly up. If I don't get back, I'll have that Athene on my tail. You ready?"

"Certainly," said Lydia, feeling more than ready.

"Well, here we are again," said Arachne's small voice. She stretched her legs in pairs, starting at the front, and working astern. Then she doodled a capital "A" in a debased Gothic script to assure herself that her spinning faculties were unimpaired.

"You know," she said, "habit is a curious thing. I'm not sure that by now I'm not more comfortable like this, after all. Less inhibited, really."

She scuttered over to the side of the bench and let herself down, looking like a ball of brilliant feathers sinking to the floor. As she reached it, she unfolded her legs, and ran across to the open door, On the threshold she paused.

"Well, good-bye, and thanks a lot," she said. "I'm sorry about your husband. I'm afraid I rather forgot myself for the moment."

Then she scooted away down the passage as if she were a ball of colored wools blowing away in the draught.

"Good-bye," said Lydia, by no means sorry to see her go.

The intention of Arachne's parting remark was lost on her: in fact, she forgot it altogether until she discovered the collection of extraordinary knobby bones that someone had recently put in the dustbin.

THE
SKI-LIFT

DIANA
BUTTENSHAW

Werner and Klaus came up from Innsbruck together to stay for two nights in the mountain village of Durach, and to go skiing in Hoch Durach two thousand feet higher. They had been friends once, inseparable boyhood friends. Sometimes, even now this friendship broke through again and they could be happy in each other's company; but for most of the time they were bitter rivals and hatred between them flowed in sudden spurts. They were rivals because of the beauty, the quite devastating beauty, of Brigitte Zach. They had both fallen in love with her the moment they saw her, when she first came to live in their Innsbruck street, and their friendship had fallen apart as though split by an axe.

They had only come up to Durach together because, although they both wanted to spend the weekend skiing, neither trusted the other to stay away from Innsbruck and Brigitte once out of sight. They had agreed to stay in the same

Gasthaus in Durach to go up skiing together to the snowfields of Hoch Durach, and to return by the same bus to Innsbruck.

After the months of rivalry and suspicion there was a feeling of mutual relief now they were out of Brigitte's sphere of influence. They even began to feel their way back to friendship as it had once been, to talk naturally and serenely together. They were happier than they had been for some months.

There are two ways of getting from Durach, in the valley, to Hoch Durach, high above in the mountains. One is by a track which winds and writhes its way up the slopes, twisting among the trees lower down, clinging to the bare shoulders higher up, for some three miles. Cars can get up or down this track one at a time, very slowly. The other way is by chair lift, a giant cable carrying dozens of swaying chairs over the tops of the trees, from pylon to pylon, two thousand feet up the face of the mountain. Sometimes the chairs are not far from the ground; sometimes they are thirty or forty feet up. There is something rather terrible about this chair lift when seen from below, but once in the chairs the peace and the silence take over from the fear.

Werner and Klaus arrived on Friday night and slept well in their plain, scrubbed bedroom in the Krone. In the morning they joined the queue at the foot of the chair lift, and waited their turn. When it came, the attendant wrapped a rug swiftly round Werner and swung the chair under him as it swept round the wheel and towards him. He sat back with a jerk, clutching his skis in one arm, and rose swaying away from the engine-house and up towards the woods on the slope above. Turning, with a sudden, jealous doubt, he saw Klaus behind him, and settled back, relieved. Klaus was not such a bad fellow after all. It was a pity he had to get this infatuation for Brigitte. Especially when he wasn't at all her type. Brigitte liked tall, dark men like himself; not small bouncing blond ones like Klaus. Much wiser if he acknowledged defeat and left the field clear. They could have got on so well then, Klaus could even have been best man.

The chair clattered quietly over the arms of a pylon and jerked a little, and he looked down to see the blue-shadowed snow piled on the rocks below. Now they were going over the woods, over a clearing cut between the trees to allow the chairs to pass up and down the endless cable. He could see one of the ski runs down from Hock Durach winding between the pines, the corners banked by the turning skiers. The first people were coming down already: lone experts ahead of the crowds, and the advanced classes led by instructors. Werner watched as a girl shot down a straight and swung into a perfect parallel turn beneath him, her body slim and supple. Brigitte skied like that. What a shame she could not come up this weekend, held in Innsbruck by some dull relation or other down from Vienna.

The cable ran over a quarry, buried now in the snow, but deep and hollow below. Then it dipped into the trees again, so that they were dark on either side. The sun did not reach the valley except at midday, and Werner clutched the rug against his stomach, feeling the chill creep into him.

Behind him Klaus regarded his back with complacency. No risk of Werner stealing a march on him, no chance of finding that he had slipped off to see Brigitte alone as he had that day last month when they had gone with a crowd to watch ski-jumping on the great Olympic jump. Werner had been a good chap once: a true friend. But one couldn't trust him anymore. Not that he had a chance with Brigitte, he was too dour, not gay and carefree as he was himself.

The chairs ran suddenly into sunlight, out over the snow slopes above the trees. Above them lay the scattered chalets and hotels of Hock Durach and the vast, white spread of glittering snow flowing up to the peaks of the mountains, tremendous against a blue sky. There were people everywhere already, flashing like swallows round the humps and curves of snow, or stumbling slowly in line in classes on the nursery slopes.

The attendant at the top whisked away the blankets as they stepped out of the chairs and clear of them, and the chairs swung round the wheel and downwards again towards Durach.

Werner waited for Klaus, and they walked together along the track towards a shorter lift which took them even higher up the huge snowslopes. Then they skied swiftly downwards together, laughing in the wine-clear air, their skis hissing in the soft, new snow, the sun warming their faces.

They stayed up on the slopes all morning, speeding down to Hoch Durach and traveling up on the short lift several times to keep in the sun. They found themselves more and more in accord, and when they raced it was amicably, without bitter rivalry. As the sun warmed their glowing bodies, so their hearts warmed too, and they forgot the arid months which lay immediately behind them, and remembered the gleaming years before, when their friendship had been a most splendid thing. They even forgot Brigitte.

They had lunch at the Alpenblich, with tall glasses of beer, sitting out in the sun on the terrace. There was every sort of people there: Dutch and English, French and German, Belgian and American.

"Even some Austrians!" laughed Klaus.

There were a few people they knew from former times, but no one who knew them well enough to join them, and they were glad, enjoying being alone together again.

After lunch they ran down the fast run into Durach, and came up on the giant ski-lift again to have another. No time to waste sitting about when there were only two days in which to ski! This time they ran down the Green Run, longer than the fast run and less exacting. It was full of classes in various stages, and Werner grumbled at the delays which they imposed.

"One can never get a good free run. These beginners stand about all over the track, and bunch up at the corners. If one goes through them at all fast, the instructors curse one."

"Well, I suppose we should have stuck to the Red and the Yellow Runs, where they don't learn," remarked Klaus peaceably.

"Yes, but you get down them too fast. You do get more skiing in this one."

"We shan't have time for another tonight. The lift stops in under ten minutes," said Klaus.

"Gottdamn! We should have just made it without all these learners."

They swung round a corner together, making plans for the evening. They decided on the bar of the Golden Rose, and perhaps an hour at the dance in the Eidelweiss before bed. They were very contented in spite of the slowness of the run. Then they saw a girl ahead of them they both knew, an old school friend from Innsbruck.

"Hello Anne-Lise! We didn't know you were here!"

"Of course you didn't, with Brigitte about," she answered wryly.

"Brigitte? She isn't up here, she couldn't come," said Klaus.

"She could. She has. She came up this afternoon in her cousin's Mercedes."

"Her cousin? The old man from Vienna?" asked Werner, astonished.

"*Old* man? This isn't an old man! A pretty distant cousin,

too, I should think. Although not all that distant as a man."
Anne-Lise was fed up with Brigitte. She already had Werner
and Klaus as her slobbering slaves, and now here was this
so-called cousin, infinitely more desirable, and with a Mercedes too.

"She isn't—"

"She doesn't-"

Werner and Klaus both shouted at once.

"I should think she is and she does," snapped Anne-Lise,
and skied on.

"Stop a minute! Where is she now?" shouted Werner.

"At the Berg, I should think. They were stopping there the
night. They *said* in separate rooms."

"The Berg? That's in Hoch Durach," muttered Klaus.
"And the lift will stop in another minute or two."

Werner suddenly saw him through hostile eyes. He was
thinking of going up there, was he? Up there to cut out this
cousin. Well, why not? Only it wouldn't be Klaus who would
cut him out, but he, Werner. The lift would be closed by the
time they reached the bottom, the gates shut while the chairs
did their last run round until all were empty. The only way
would be up the three mile track. Well, that wouldn't take all
that long, and his legs were longer than Klaus'.

Klaus was thinking the same as they sped in silence down
the darkening track. Werner could stride faster on the flat, but
he was heavier. He would tire much quicker.

We shall get there almost together anyway, thought
Werner furiously. What fools we shall look, panting in, one
behind the other!

It was then that they came upon one of the pylons carrying
the chair-lift cable, looming out of the gathering dusk like the
ghost of a skeleton. The chairs were still moving, they would go
on empty for some time yet. Klaus was the first to realize its

possibility. He remembered that Werner hated heights, he had never been a climber, as Klaus was. Klaus skidded to a violent halt at the foot of the pylon, flicked off his skis in one movement, and started to climb the pylon.

"Klaus! What the hell—?" As he shouted, Werner stopped too in a flurry of snow, and then came leaping back. He was trying to steal a march, was he? Werner, too, kicked off his skis and climbed upwards, his fear of heights forgotten in his fury. Before he could reach him Klaus had leaned outwards and caught the bar of a chair as it passed, leaping outwards and jerking himself into the seat. It swung wildly beneath him, then was clear of the pylon and on its way upwards. The sweat burst suddenly out on Werner's face, then he climbed still higher, leaned out on one arm, and prepared to seize the following chair as it came past. Klaus knew he was afraid of heights: he had planneed to do this to leave him behind. Well, damn him, he was only one chair behind.

Werner landed in the swaying chair in a heap and nearly slipped out again. Then he got a firmer grip and pulled himself properly up in the seat. Ahead of him Klaus turned round and stared at him through the twilight. It was too dark to see his expression, but in the great silence of the snow Werner heard him swear aloud.

It was eerie up there, traveling alone among the trees, with no other human but each other. They must have been almost the last skiers on the slopes: no one now slipped past on the run which shone dimly through the pines: no one came past them on the downwards line of chairs.

The darkness was falling almost visibly upon them; only the snow gleamed white below them; the trees were mingling together into shadow.

The chairs rose on the cable away from the ground a little, riding over a dell between two pylons.

Then they slowed down, and stopped.

For a moment both Klaus and Werner waited for them to start again, assuming some hitch, some temporary fault. Then as the chairs hung motionless in the silence they realized that they had misjudged the time. The lift had stopped for the night.

"Damn!" thought Klaus. "We shall have to shout." Then he remembered that neither the road nor the ski run came near this section of the lift.

"There'll be some instructors coming down after the classes," thought Werner. They wouldn't be too pleased at having to start up the lift again. There was a heavy fine for getting on illegally. It was all Klaus' fault. Then, he, too, remembered that the run was some way off.

"They'll hear if we shout," he called to Klaus, hating having to communicate with him. "If we both shout together."

They called in unison, yodeling at intervals as well. But with the darkness a light wind had got up, and their shouts did not carry to the distant ski run, if, indeed, anyone were on it so late. Both the top and bottom stations were too far away, and the curves of the mountains hid them.

Werner looked back to see how near the pylon behind him was, but it was quite a distance.

"Are you near the next pylon?" he called, forgetting for a moment his anger.

"Yards away, and all uphill. Can you reach yours?"

Werner looked up at the slender tube that held the chair to the cable. It would be slippery, and icy cold. The cable itself was thin: it would cut into one's hands, even if he had the courage to dangle there above the depths.

"Not a hope!" he answered

They sat there in silence, listening and listening. There was nothing moving, nothing in all the great emptiness of sky and mountain and snow. The wind stirred again in the trees, moaning through them and whispering round the cables, cutting into their bodies. Then it went, leaving only the still, cold air and the silence again.

"Shout now!"

Their voices rang out, shattering the peace, but there was no one to hear, no answer.

Even with the blankets normally wrapped round one, this lift was always a cold one, traveling so high, and for so long. Without the blankets the cold crept into their bellies and ran down their spines, chilling their arms and legs.

Colder and colder. More and more silent. Silent and still and cold.

Klaus looked down. The slope could not be very far away, and there would be two or three feet of snow. If he made a rope of his anorak and jersey the ground would be even nearer. Without them he would be bitterly cold, but he would warm up moving. Not easy to move in deep snow without skis. But better than sitting up here, waiting for help that was unlikely to come, and freezing. He took off his anorak and knotted one sleeve round the stanchion of the chair, then removed his jersey and tied an arm to the other arm of the anorak. Would they hold? Would one material slide out of the other? He pulled; they seemed firm enough. Without them his body was chilling so rapidly that his heart gave a lurch of fear.

From behind him Werner watched the movements in the darkness, silhouetted against the snow of the slope. What was Klaus doing? The shadow elongated as Klaus slid down off the seat, fumbling his way down the straining garments.

"Damn him!" breathed Werner. "He's getting a start on me again! He'll get to Brigitte first!" He watched, holding his breath.

Klaus felt his way down, the material stretching and awkward to his grasp. He could feel the knot beginning to give way. He would have to jump now; to let go as he reached the end of his rope before it broke. The ground couldn't be all that far.

He let go, falling, falling, far farther than he had expected. The rocks hit him in a blinding, smashing, flaming sheet of pain which engulfed him and tore away his senses.

Werner saw him fall, heard the cracking thud as he hit the rocks beneath the snow.

There was no sound for five minutes. Nothing. Then the moaning began, high and thin, inhuman in the still air.

As Klaus regained consciousness he knew that both legs were broken, utterly smashed and useless. They were not numb, he could feel them, feel them and hear the bones grating when he tried to move out of his agonizing position. He could hear the same high keening that Werner heard, not understanding at first that it was his own voice. As his mind cleared he cried louder, shouting to Werner to help him, to stop this fearful pain that beat and hammered at him, drowning him in wave after wave.

"Werner! Werner! Help me! Help me!" but Werner sat immobile with horror and hate and fear, staring at the shadow which lay dark against the white snow, his teeth chattering together.

It was Klaus' fault! He had tried to get down first and up to Brigitte. It was he who had led the way up the pylon into this frightful lift. It was all his fault, and now he, Werner, was stuck up here, and no one to help him. Why couldn't Klaus fetch help? Why couldn't he pull himself through the trees to the road?

The moaning rose and fell, wailing through the silence, ghostly and thin.

"Shut up! Shut up!"

Klaus did not hear him. The cold was driving into him

through the thinness of his shirt, up the shattered bones of his legs. Already the blood that ran down them had clotted and frozen, no longer running away. Already the pain that engulfed him was changing, eating into his spine and through his entrails, up into his chest. He could hear the wailing still, but thinner, fainter. Whoever was crying was moving farther away. Farther and farther.

When he had lain there for an hour the thin sound faded away altogether. The silence returned to the snow and the waiting trees.

When it had utterly ceased Werner longed for its return.

He was alone now. Klaus had left him alone. With the silence he remembered that he and Klaus had been friends. Only a few hours ago they had been friends again. They had done so much together. Now Klaus had gone away and left him, and he was alone.

No rival for Brigitte now, he thought suddenly. Only the cousin.

All the same, he would rather Klaus had not left him alone.

He sat there, stiffening in the silent cold, watching the still shadow in the snow. He would have to move soon: no use waiting much longer. No one would come now.

Once or twice he looked up at the support above him, measuring the distance to the cable. Then it would be hand over hand down the wire to the pylon. Must get his hands warm first, or he would never hold on. Fall, like Klaus. Keep his hands very still, warmer that way. Not move them on the cold wood of the chair. Keep very still, warm patch between his legs. No, not warm, but not so cold as the rest of him. Move his hands in between his legs. No—keep still. Moving made things colder. Lost heat that way. Keep very still.

He stared at the shadow that had been Klaus. No use

going down that way. Must go upwards. Someone might come quite soon. The chairs might start again, moving up and away from the shadow in the snow. Getting colder and colder, right down in the belly, all through. No good moving. Stay very still and get warm.

Poor Klaus.

Rather have Klaus than Brigitte.

The stars coming closer now, right down among the mountains, down among the waiting trees. Pressing down the cold, and the peaks of the mountains leaning over, closing in the cold.

Keep still. Keep still. Keep still.

Werner did get to the top first. When the lift started moving in the morning the attendant at Hoch Durach was surprised to see the first passenger of the day arriving some ten minutes sooner than he expected anyone. He was even more surprised when, as this first passenger drew nearer, he stared clean through him with wide, blue eyes. But his greatest shock came when he seized one arm to help him get out of the chair. The arm was as stiff and as rigid as wood.

Brigitte married the cousin. She had never intended doing anything else.

THE
BEETLES

ROBERT
BLOCH

When Hartley returned from Egypt, his friends said he had changed. The specific nature of that change was difficult to detect, for none of his acquaintances got more than a casual glimpse of him. He dropped around to the club just once, and then retired to the seclusion of his apartments. His manner was so definitely hostile, so markedly anti-social, that very few of his cronies cared to visit him, and the occasional callers were not received.

It caused considerable talk at the time—gossip rather. Those who remembered Arthur Hartley in the days before his expedition abroad were naturally quite cut up over the drastic metamorphosis in his manner. Hartley had been known as a keen scholar, a singularly erudite fieldworker in his chosen profession of archaeology: but at the same time he had been a peculiarly charming person. He had the worldly flair usually associated with the fictional characters of E. Phillips Oppenheim, and a positively devilish sense of humor which mocked and belittled it. He was the kind of fellow who could order the precise wine at the proper moment, at the same time grinning as though he were as much surprised by it all as his guest of the evening. And most of his friends found this air of culture without ostentation quite engaging. He had carried this urbane sense of the ridiculous over into his work; and while it was known that he was very much interested in archaeology, and a notable figure in the field, he inevitably referred to his studies as "pottering around with old fossils and the old fossils that discovered them."

Consequently, his curious reversal following his trip came as a complete surprise.

All that was definitely known was that he had spent some eight months on a field trip to the Egyptian Sudan. Upon his return he had immediately severed all connections with the institute he had been associated with. Just what had occurred during the expedition was a matter of excited conjecture among his former intimates. But something had definitely happened; it was unmistakable.

The night he spent at the club proved that. He had come in quietly, too quietly. Hartley was one of those persons who usually made an entrance, in the true sense of the word. His tall, graceful figure, attired in the immaculate evening dress so seldom found outside of the pages of melodramatic fiction: his truly leonine head with its Stokowski-like bristle of gray hair: these attributes commanded attention. He could have passed anywhere as a man of the world, or a stage magician awaiting his cue to step onto the platform.

But this evening he entered quietly, unobtrusively. He wore dinner clothes, but his shoulders sagged, and the spring was gone from his walk. His hair was grayer, and it hung pallidly over his tanned forehead. Despite the bronze of Egyptian sun on his features, there was a sickly tinge to his countenance. His eyes peered mistily from amidst unsightly folds. His face seemed to have lost its mold; the mouth hung loosely.

He greeted no one, and took a table alone. Of course cronies came up and chatted, but he did not invite them to join him. And oddly enough, none of them insisted, although normally they would gladly have forced their company upon him and jollied him out of a black mood, which experience had taught them was easily done in his case. Nevertheless, after a few words with Hartley, they all turned away.

They must have felt it even then. Some of them hazarded the opinion that Hartley was still suffering from some form of fever contracted in Egypt, but I do not think they believed this in their hearts. From their shocked description of the man they seemed one and all to sense the peculiar *alien* quality about him. This was an Arthur Hartley they had never known, an aged stranger, with a querulous voice which rose in suspicion when he was questioned about his journey. Stranger he truly was, for he did not even appear to recognize some of the men who greeted him, and when he did it was with an abstracted manner—a clumsy way of wording it, but what else is there to say when an old friend stares blankly into silence upon meeting, and his eyes seem to fasten on far-off terrors that affright him?

That was the strangeness they all grasped in Hartley. He was afraid. Fear bestrode those sagging shoulders. Fear breathed a pallor into that ashy face. Fear grinned into those empty, far-fixed eyes. Fear prompted the suspicion in the voice.

They told me, and that is why I went around to see Arthur

Hartley in his rooms. Others had spoken of their efforts, in the week following his appearance at the club, to gain admittance to his apartment. They said he did not answer the bell, and complained that the phone had been disconnected. But that, I reasoned, was fear's work.

I wouldn't let Hartley down. I had been a rather good friend of his—and I may as well confess that I scented a mystery here. The combination proved irresistible. I went up to his flat one afternoon and rang.

No answer. I went into the dim hallway and listened for footsteps, some sign of life from within. No answer. Complete, utter silence. For a moment I thought crazily of suicide, then laughed the dread away. It was absurd—and still, there had been a certain dismayed unanimity in all the reports I had heard of Hartley's mental state. When the stolidest, most hardheaded of the club bores concurred in their estimate of the man's condition, I might well worry. Still, suicide...

I rang again, more as a gesture than in expectation of tangible results, and then I turned and descended the stairs. I felt, I recall, a little twinge of inexplicable relief upon leaving the place. The thought of suicide in that gloomy hallway had not been pleasant.

I reached the lower door and opened it, and a familiar figure scurried past me on the landing. I turned. It was Hartley.

For the first time since his return I got a look at the man, and in the hallway shadows he was ghastly. Whatever his condition at the club, a week must have accentuated it tremendously. His head was lowered, and as I greeted him he looked up. His eyes gave me a terrific shock. There was a stranger dwelling in their depths—a haunted stranger. I swear he shook when I addressed him.

He was wearing a tattered topcoat, but it hung loosely

over his gauntness. I noticed that he was carrying a large bundle done up in brown paper.

I said something. I don't remember what: at any rate, I was at some pains to conceal my confusion as I greeted him. I was rather insistently cordial, I believe, for I could see that he would just have soon have hurried up the stairs without even speaking to me. The astonishment I felt converted itself into heartiness. Rather reluctantly he invited me up.

We entered the flat, and I noticed that Hartley double-locked the door behind him. That, to me, characterized his metamorphosis. In the old days, Hartley had always kept open house, in the literal sense of the word. Studies might have kept him late at the institute, but a chance visitor found his door open wide. And now, he double-locked it.

I turned around and surveyed the apartment. Just what I expected to see I cannot say, but certainly my mind was prepared for some sign of radical alteration. There was none. The furniture had not been moved; the pictures hung in their original place; the vast bookcases still stood in the shadows.

Hartley excused himself, entered the bedroom, and presently emerged after discarding his topcoat. Before he sat down he walked over to the mantel and struck a match before a little bronze figurine of Horus. A second later the thick gray spirals of smoke arose in the approved style of exotic fiction, and I smelled the pungent tang of strong incense.

That was the first puzzler. I had unconsciously adopted the attitude of a detective looking for clues—or, perhaps, a psychiatrist ferreting out psychoneurotic tendencies. And the incense was definitely alien to the Arthur Hartley I knew.

"Clears away the smell," he remarked.

I didn't ask "What smell?" Nor did I begin to question him as to his trip, his inexplicable conduct in not answering my correspondence after he left Khartoum, or his avoidance of my company in this week following his return. Instead, I let him talk.

He said nothing at first. His conversation rambled, and behind it all I sensed the abstraction I had been warned about. He spoke of having given up his work, and hinted that he might leave the city shortly and go up to his family home in the country. He had been ill. He was disappointed in Egyptology, and its limitations. He hated darkness. The locust plagues had increased in Kansas.

This rambling was—insane.

I knew it then, and I hugged the thought to me in the perverse delight which is born of dread. Hartley was mad. "Limitations" of Egyptology. "I hate the dark." "The locusts of Kansas."

But I sat silently when he lighted the great candles about the room; sat silently staring through the incense clouds to where the flaming tapers illuminated his twitching features. And then he broke.

"You are my friend?" he said. There was a question in his voice, a puzzled suspicion in his words that brought sudden pity to me. His derangement was terrible to witness. Still, I nodded gravely.

"You are my friend," he continued. This time the words were a statement. The deep breath which followed betokened resolution on his part.

"Do you know what was in that bundle I brought in?" he asked suddenly.

"No."

"I'll tell you. Insecticide. *That's* what it was. Insecticide!"

His eyes flamed in triumph which stabbed me.

"I haven't left this house for a week. I dare not spread the plague. They follow me, you know. But today I thought of the way—absurdly simple, too. I went out and bought insecticide. Pounds of it. And liquid spray. Special formula stuff, more deadly than arsenic. Just elementary science, really—but its very prosaicness may defeat the Powers of Evil."

I nodded like a fool, wondering whether I could arrange for him to be taken away that evening. Perhaps my friend, Doctor Sherman, might diagnose...

"Now let them come! It's my last chance—the incense doesn't work, and even if I keep the lights burning they creep about the corners. Funny the woodwork holds up; it should be riddled."

What was this?

"But I forgot," said Hartley. "You don't know about it. The plague, I mean. And the curse." He leaned forward and his white hands made octopus-shadows on the wall.

"I used to laugh at it, you know," he said. "Archaeology isn't exactly a pursuit for the superstitious. Too much grovelling in ruins. And putting curses on old pottery and battered statues never seemed important to me. But Egyptology—that's different. It's human bodies, there. Mummified, but still human. And the Egyptians were a great race—they had scientific secrets we haven't yet fathomed, and of course we cannot even begin to approach their concepts in mysticism."

Ah! There was the key! I listened, intently.

"I learned a lot, this last trip. We were after the excavation job in the new tombs up the river. I brushed up on the dynastic periods, and naturally the religious significance entered into it. Oh, I know all the myths—the Bubatis legend, the Isis resurrection, the names of Ra, the allegory of Set—

"We found things there, in the tombs—wonderful things. The pottery, the furniture, the bas-reliefs we were able to remove. But the expeditionary reports will be out soon; you can read of it then. We found mummies, too . . . cursed mummies."

Now I saw it all, or thought I did.

"And I was a fool. I did something I never should have dared to do—for ethical reasons, and for other, more important reasons. Reasons that may cost me my soul."

I had to keep my grip on myself, remember that he was mad, remember that his convincing tones were prompted by the delusions of insanity. Or else, in that dark room I might have easily believed that there was a power which had driven my friend to his hazzard brink.

"Yes, I did it, I tell you! I read the Curse of Scarabaeus— sacred beetles, you know—and I did it anyway. I couldn't guess that it was true. I was a sceptic; everyone is sceptical enough until things happen. Those things are like the phenomenon of death; you read about it, realize that it occurs to others, and yet cannot quite conceive of it happening to yourself. And yet it does. The Curse of the Scarabaeus was like that."

Thoughts of the Sacred Beetle of Egypt crossed my mind. And I remembered, also, the seven plagues. And I knew what he would say. . . .

"We came back. On the ship I noticed them. They crawled out of the corners every night. When I turned the light on they went away, but they always returned when I tried to sleep. I burned incense to keep them off, and then I moved into a new cabin. But they followed me.

"I did not dare tell anyone. Most of the chaps would have laughed and the Egyptologists in the party wouldn't have helped much. Besides, I couldn't confess my crime. So I went on alone."

His voice was a dry whisper.

"It was pure hell. One night on the boat I saw the black

things crawling in my food. After that I ate in the cabin, alone. I dared not see anyone now, for fear they might notice how the things followed me. They did follow me, you know—if I walked in shadow on the deck they crept along behind. Only the sun kept them back, or a pure flame. I nearly went mad trying to account logically for their presence, trying to imagine how they got on the boat. But all the time I knew in my heart what the truth was. They were a sending—the Curse!

"When I reached port I went up and resigned. When my guilt was discovered there would have been a scandal, anyway, so I resigned. I couldn't hope to continue work with those things crawling all over, wherever I went. I was afraid to look anyone up. Naturally, I tried. That one night at the club was ghastly, though—I could see them marching across the carpet and crawling up the sides of my chair, and it took all there was in me to keep me from screaming and dashing out.

"Since then I've stayed here, alone. Before I decide on any course for the future, I must fight the Curse and win. Nothing else will help."

I started to interject a phrase, but he brushed it aside and continued desperately.

"No, I couldn't go away. They followed me across the ocean; they haunt me in the streets. I could be locked up and they would still come. They come every night and crawl up the sides of my bed and try to get at my face and I must sleep soon or I'll go mad; they crawl over my face at night, they crawl—"

It was horrible to see the words come out between his set teeth, for he was fighting madly to control himself.

"Perhaps the insecticide will kill them. It was the first thing I should have thought of, but of course panic confused me. Yes, I put my trust in the insecticide. Grotesque, isn't it? Fighting an ancient curse with insect powder?"

I spoke at last. "They're beetles, aren't they?"

He nodded. "Scarabaeus beetles. You know the curse. The mummies under the protection of the Scarab cannot be violated."

I knew the curse. It was one of the oldest known to history. Like all legends, it had a persistent life. Perhaps I could reason.

"But why should it affect *you*?" I asked. Yes, I would reason with Hartley. Egyptian fever had deranged him, and the colorful curse story had gripped his mind. If I spoke logically, I might get him to understand his hallucination. "Why should it affect you?" I repeated.

He was silent for a moment before he spoke, and then his words seemed to be wrung out of him.

"I stole a mummy," he said. "I stole the mummy of a temple virgin. I must have been crazy to do it; something happens to you under that sun. There was gold in the case, and jewels, and ornaments. And there was the Curse, written. I got them—both."

I stared at him, and knew that in this he spoke the truth.

"That's why I cannot keep up my work. I stole the mummy, and I am cursed. I didn't believe, but the crawling things came just as the inscription said.

"At first I thought that was the meaning of the Curse, that wherever I went the beetles would go, too, that they would haunt me and keep me from men forever. But lately I am beginning to think differently. I think the beetles will act as messengers of vengeance. I think they mean to kill me."

This was pure raving.

"I haven't dared open the mummy case since. I'm afraid to read the inscription again. I have it here in the house, but I've locked it up and I won't show you. I want to burn it—but I must keep it on hand. In a way, it's the only proof of my sanity. And if the things kill me—"

"Snap out of it," I commanded. Then I started. I don't know the exact words I used, but I said reassuring, hearty, wholesome things. And when I finished he smiled the martyred smile of the obsessed.

"Delusions? They're real. But where do they come from? I can't find any cracks in the woodwork. The walls are sound. And yet every night the beetles come and crawl up the bed and try to get at my face. They don't bite, they merely crawl. There are thousands of them—black thousands of silent crawling things, inches long. I brush them away, but when I fall asleep they come back, they're clever, and I can't pretend. I've never caught one; they're too fast-moving. They seem to understand me—or the Power that sends them understands.

"They crawl up from Hell night after night, and I can't last much longer. Some evening, I'll fall completely asleep and they will creep over my face and then—"

He leaped to his feet and screamed.

"The corner—in the corner now—out of the walls—"

The black shadows were moving, marching.

I saw a blur, fancied I could detect rustling forms advancing, creeping, spreading before the light.

Hartley sobbed.

I turned on the electric light. There was, of course, nothing there. I didn't say a word, but left abruptly. Hartley continued to sit huddled in his chair, his head in his hands.

I went straight to my friend, Doctor Sherman.

He diagnosed it as I thought he would, phobia, accompanied by hallucinations. Hartley's feeling of guilt over stealing the mummy haunted him. The visions of beetles resulted.

All this Sherman studded with the mumbo-jumbo technicalities of the professional psychiatrist, but it was simple enough. Together we phoned the institute where Hartley had worked. They verified the story, insofar as they knew Hartley had stolen a mummy.

After dinner Sherman had an appointment, but he promised to meet me at ten and go with me again to Hartley's apartment. I was quite insistent about this, for I felt that there was no time to lose. Of course, this was a mawkish attitude on my part, but that strange afternoon session had deeply disturbed me.

I spent the early evening in unnerving reflection. Perhaps that was the way all so-called "Egyptian curses" worked. A guilty conscience on the part of a tomb-looter made him project the shadow of imaginary punishment on himself. He had hallucinations of retribution. That might explain the mysterious Tut-ankh-amen deaths; it certainly accounted for the suicides.

And that was why I insisted on Sherman seeing Hartley that same night. I feared suicide very much, for if ever a man was on the verge of complete mental collapse, Arthur Hartley surely was.

It was nearly eleven, however, before Sherman and I rang the bell. There was no answer. We stood in the dark hallway as I vainly rapped, then pounded. The silence only served to augment my anxiety. I was truly afraid, or else I never would have dared use my skeleton key.

As it was, I felt the end justified the means. We entered.

The living room was bare of occupants. Nothing had changed since the afternoon—I could see that quite clearly, for all the lights were on, and the guttering candle-stumps still smouldered.

Both Sherman and I smelled the reek of the insecticide quite strongly, and the floor was almost evenly coated with thick white insect powder.

We called, of course, before I ventured to enter the bedroom. It was dark, and I thought it was empty until I turned on the lights and saw the figure huddled beneath the bedclothes. It was Arthur Hartley, and I needed no second glance to see that his white face was twisted in death.

The reek of insecticide was stronger here and incense burned; and yet there was another pungent smell—a musty odor, vaguely animal-like.

Sherman stood at my side, staring.

"What shall we do?" I asked.

"I'll get the police on the wire downstairs," he said. "Touch nothing."

He dashed out, and I followed him from the room, sickened. I could not bear to approach the body of my friend— that hideous expression on the face affrighted me. Suicide, murder, heart attack—I didn't even wish to know the manner of his passing. I was heartsick to think that we had been too late.

I turned from the bedroom and then that damnable scent came to my nostrils redoubled, and I knew. "Beetles!"

But how could there be beetles? It was all an illusion in poor Hartley's brain. Even his twisted mind had realized that there were no apertures in the walls to admit them, that they could not be seen about the place.

And still the smell rose on the air—the reek of death, of decay, of ancient corruption that reigned in Egypt. I followed the scent to the second bedroom, forced the door.

On the bed lay the mummy case. Hartley had said he locked it up in here. The lid was closed, but ajar.

I opened it. The sides bore inscriptions, and one of them may have pertained to the Scarabaeus Curse. I do not know, for I stared only at the ghastly, unshrouded figure that lay within. It was a mummy, and it had been sucked dry. It was all shell. There was a great cavity in the stomach, and as I peered within I could see a few feebly crawling forms—inch long, black buttons with great writhing feelers. They shrank back in the light, but not before I saw the scarab patterns on the outer crusted backs.

The secret of the Curse was here—the beetles had dwelt within the body of the mummy! They had eaten it out and nested within, and at night they crawled forth. It was true then!

I screamed once when the thought hit me, and dashed back to Hartley's bedroom. I could hear the sound of footsteps ascending the outer stairs; the police were on their way, but I couldn't wait. I raced into the bedroom, dread tugging at my heart.

Had Hartley's story been true, after all? Were the beetles really messengers of a divine vengeance?

I ran into that bedroom where Arthur Hartley lay, stooped over his huddled figure on the bed. My hands fumbled over the body, searching for a wound. I had to know how he had died.

But there was no blood, there was no mark, and there was no weapon beside him. It had been shock or heart attack, after all. I was strangely relieved when I thought of this. I stood up and eased the body back again on the pillows.

Where were they now? They had left the mummy and disappeared, and Hartley was dead. Where were they?

Suddenly I stared again at Hartley. There was something wrong with that body on the bed. When I had lifted the corpse it seemed singularly light for a man of Hartley's build. As I gazed at him now, he seemed empty of more than life. I peered into that ravaged face more closely, and then I shuddered. For the cords of his neck moved convulsively, his chest seemed to rise and fall, his head fell sideways on the pillow. He lived—or something inside him did!

And then as his twisted features moved, I cried aloud, for I knew how Hartley had died, and what had killed him; knew the secret of the Scarab Curse and why the beetles crawled out of the mummy to seek his bed. I knew what they had meant to do—what, tonight, they had done. I cried aloud as I saw Hartley's face move, in hopes that my voice would drown that dreadful rustling sound which filled the room and came *from inside Hartley's body.*

I knew that the Scarab Curse had killed him, and I screamed quite wildly as the mouth gaped slowly open. Just as I fainted, I saw Arthur Hartley's dead lips part, allowing a rustling swarm of *black Scarabaeus beetles* to pour out across the pillow.

HIS UNCONQUERABLE ENEMY

W.C. MORROW

I was summoned from Calcutta to the heart of India to perform a difficult surgical operation on one of the women of a great rajah's household. I found the rajah a man of a noble character, but possessed, as I afterward discovered, of a sense of cruelty purely Oriental and in contrast to the indolence of his disposition. He was so grateful for the success that attended my mission that he urged me to remain a guest at the palace as long as it might please me to stay, and I thankfully accepted the invitation.

One of the male servants attracted my notice for his marvelous capacity of malice. His name was Neranya, and I am certain that there must have been a large proportion of Malay blood in his veins. He was extremely alert, active, nervous, and sensitive. A redeeming circumstance was his love for his master. Once his violent temper led him to the commission of an atrocious crime—the fatal stabbing of a dwarf. In punishment for this the rajah ordered that Neranya's right arm (the offending one) be severed from his body. The sentence was executed in a bungling fashion by a stupid fellow armed with an axe, and I, being a surgeon, was compelled, in order to save Neranya's life, to perform an amputation of the stump, leaving not a vestige of the limb remaining.

After this he developed an augmented fiendishness. His love for the rajah was changed to hate, and in his mad anger he flung discretion to the winds. Driven once to frenzy by the rajah's scornful treatment, he sprang upon the rajah with a knife, but, fortunately, was seized and disarmed. To his unspeakable dismay the rajah sentenced him for this offence to suffer amputation of the remaining arm. It was done as in the former instance. This had the effect of putting a temporary curb on Neranya's spirit, or, rather, of changing outward manifestations of his diabolism.

Being armless, he was at first largely at the mercy of those who ministered to his needs—a duty which I undertook to see was properly discharged, for I felt an interest in this strangely distorted nature. His sense of helplessness, combined with a damnable scheme for revenge which he had secretly formed, caused Neranya to change his fierce, impetuous, and unruly conduct into a smooth, quiet, insinuating bearing, which he carried so artfully as to deceive those with whom he was brought in contact, including the rajah himself.

Neranya, being exceedingly quick, intelligent, and dexterous, and having an unconquerable will, turned his attention to the cultivating of an enlarged usefulness of his legs, feet, and toes, with so excellent effect that in time he was able to perform wonderful feats with those members. Thus his capability, especially for destructive mischief, was considerably restored.

One morning the rajah's only son, a young man of an uncommonly amiable and noble disposition, was found dead in bed. His murder was a most atrocious one, his body being mutilated in a shocking manner, but in my eyes the most significant of all the mutilations was the entire removal and disappearance of the young prince's arms.

The death of the young man nearly brought the rajah to the grave. It was not, therefore, until I had nursed him back to health that I began a systematic inquiry into the murder. I said nothing of my own discoveries and conclusions until after the rajah and his officers had failed and my work had been done; then I submitted to him a written report, making a close analysis of all the circumstances, and closing by charging the crime to Neranya. The rajah, convinced by my proof and argument, at once ordered Neranya to be put to death, this to be accomplished slowly and with frightful tortures. The sentence was so cruel and revolting that it filled me with horror, and I implored that the wretch be shot. Finally, through a sense of gratitude to me, the rajah relaxed. When Neranya was charged with the crime he denied it, of course, but, seeing that the rajah was convinced, he threw aside all restraint, and, dancing, laughing, and shrieking in the most horrible manner, confessed his guilt, gloated over it, and reviled the rajah to his teeth—this, knowing that some fearful death awaited him.

The rajah decided upon the details of the matter that night, and in the morning he informed me of his decision. It was that Neranya's life should be spared, but that both of his legs should be broken with hammers, and that then I should amputate the limbs at the trunk! Appended to this horrible sentence was a provision that the maimed wretch should be kept and tortured at regular intervals by such means as afterward might be devised.

Sickened to the heart by the awful duty set out for me, I nevertheless performed it with success, and I care to say nothing more about that part of the tragedy. Neranya escaped death very narrowly and was a long time in recovering his wonted vitality. During all these weeks the rajah neither saw him nor made inquiries concerning him, but when, as in duty bound, I made official report that the man had recovered his strength, the rajah's eyes brightened, and he emerged with deadly activity from the stupor into which he so long had been plunged.

The rajah's palace was a noble structure, but it is necessary here to describe only the grand hall. It was an immense chamber, with a floor of polished, inlaid stone and a lofty, arched ceiling. A soft light stole into it through stained glass set in the roof and in high windows on one side. In the middle of the room was a rich fountain, which threw up a tall, slender column of water, with smaller and shorter jets grouped around it. Across one end of the hall, halfway to the ceiling, was a balcony, which communicated with the upper story of a wing, and from which a flight of stone stairs descended to the floor of the hall. During the hot summers this room was delightfully cool; it was the rajah's favorite lounging place, and when the nights were hot he had his cot taken thither, and there he slept.

This hall was chosen for Neranya's permanent prison; here was he to stay so long as he might live, with never a glimpse of the shining world or the glorious heavens. To one of his nervous, discontented nature such confinement was worse than death. At the rajah's order there was constructed for him a small pen of open ironwork, circular, and about four feet in diameter, elevated on four slender iron posts, ten feet above the floor, and placed between the balcony and the fountain. Such was Neranya's prison. The pen was about four feet in depth, and the pen top was left open for the convenience of the servants whose duty it should be to care for him. These precautions for his safe confinement were taken at my suggestion, for, although the man was now deprived of all four of his limbs, I still feared that he might develop some extraordinary, unheard-of power for mischief. It was provided that the attendant should reach his cage by means of a movable ladder.

All these arrangements having been made, and Neranya hoisted into his cage, the rajah emerged upon the balcony to see him for the first time since the last amputation. Neranya had been lying panting and helpless on the floor of his cage, but when his quick ear caught the sound of the rajah's footfall he squirmed about until he had brought the back of his head against the railing, elevating his eyes above his chest, and enabling him to peer through the openwork of the cage. Thus the two deadly enemies faced each other. The rajah's stern face paled at the sight of the hideous, shapeless thing which met his gaze; but he soon recovered, and the old hard, cruel, sinister look returned. Neranya's black hair and beard had grown long, and they added to the natural ferocity of his aspect. His eyes blazed upon the rajah with a terrible light, his lips parted, and he gasped for breath; his face was ashen with rage and despair, and his thin, distended nostrils quivered.

The rajah folded his arms and gazed down from the balcony upon the frightful wreck that he had made. Oh, the dreadful pathos of that picture; the inhumanity of it; the deep and dismal tragedy of it! Who might look into the wild, despairing heart of the prisoner and see and understand the frightful turmoil there; the surging, choking passion; unbridled but impotent ferocity; frantic thirst for a vengeance that should be deeper than hell! Neranya gazed, his shapeless body heaving, his eyes aflame; and then, in a strong, clear voice, which rang throughout the great hall, with rapid speech he hurled at the rajah the most insulting defiance, the most awful curses. He cursed the womb that had conceived him, the food that should nourish him, the wealth that had brought him power; cursed him in the name of Buddha and all the wise men; cursed by the sun, the moon, and the stars; by the continents, mountains, oceans, and rivers; by all things living; cursed his head, his heart, his entrails; cursed in a whirlwind of unmentionable words; heaped unimaginable insults and contumely upon him; called him a knave, a beast, a fool, a liar, an infamous and unspeakable coward.

The rajah heard it all calmly, without the movement of a muscle, without the slightest change of countenance; and when the poor wretch had exhausted his strength and fallen helpless and silent to the floor, the rajah, with a grim, cold smile, turned and strode away.

The days passed. The rajah, not deterred by Neranya's curses often heaped upon him, spent even more time than formerly in the great hall, and slept there oftener at night; and finally Neranya wearied of cursing and defying him, and fell into a sullen silence. The man was a study for me, and I observed every change in his fleeting moods. Generally his condition was that of miserable despair, which he attempted bravely to conceal. Even the boon of suicide had been denied him, for when he would wriggle into an erect position the rail of his pen was a foot above his head, so that he could not clamber over and break his skull on the stone floor beneath; and when he had tried to starve himself the attendants forced food down his throat; so that he abandoned such attempts. At times his eyes would blaze and his breath would come in gasps, for imaginary vengeance was working within him; but steadily he became quieter and more tractable, and was pleasant and responsive when I would converse with him. Whatever might have been the tortures which the rajah had decided on, none as yet had been ordered; and although Neranya knew that they were in contemplation, he never referred to them or complained of his lot.

The awful climax of this situation was reached one night, and even after this lapse of years I cannot approach its description without a shudder.

It was a hot night, and the rajah had gone to sleep in the great hall, lying on a high cot placed on the main floor just underneath the edge of the balcony. I had been unable to sleep in my own apartment, and so I had stolen into the great hall through the heavily curtained entrance at the end farthest from the balcony. As I entered I heard a peculiar, soft sound above the patter of the fountain. Neranya's cage was partly concealed from my view by the spraying water, but I suspected that the unusual sound came from him. Stealing a little to one side, and crouching against the dark hangings of the wall, I could see him in the faint light which dimly illuminated the hall, and then I discovered that my surmise was correct—Neranya was quietly at work. Curious to learn more, and knowing that only mischief could have been inspiring him, I sank into a thick robe on the floor and watched him.

To my great astonishment Neranya was tearing off with his teeth the bag which served as his outer garment. He did it cautiously, casting sharp glances frequently at the rajah, who, sleeping soundly on his cot below, breathed heavily. After starting a strip with his teeth, Neranya, by the same means, would attach it to the railing of his cage and then wriggle away, much after the manner of a caterpillar's crawling, and this would cause the strip to be torn out the full length of his garment. He repeated this operation with incredible patience and skill until his entire garment had been torn into strips. Two or three of these he tied end to end with his teeth, lips, and tongue, tightening the knots by placing one end of the strip under his body and drawing the other taut with this teeth. In this way he made a line several feet long, one end of which he made fast to the rail with his mouth. It then began to dawn upon me that he was going to make an insane attempt— impossible of achievement without hands, feet, arms, or legs— to escape from his cage! For what purpose? The rajah was asleep in the hall—ah! I caught my breath. Oh, the desperate, insane thirst for revenge which could have unhinged so clear and firm a mind! Even though he should accomplish the impossible feat of climbing over the railing of his cage that he might fall to the floor below (for how could he slide down the rope?), he would be in all probability killed or stunned; and even if he should escape these dangers, it would be impossible for him to clamber upon the cot without rousing the rajah, and impossible even though the rajah were dead! Amazed at the man's daring, and convinced that his sufferings and brooding had destroyed his reason, nevertheless I watched him with breathless interest.

With other strips tied together he made a short swing across one side of his cage. He caught the long line in his teeth at a point not far from the rail; then, wriggling with great effort to an upright position, his back braced against the rail, he put his chin over the swing and worked toward one end. He tightened the grasp of his chin on the swing, and with tremendous exertion, working the lower end of his spine against the railing, he began gradually to ascend the side of his cage. The labor was so great that he was compelled to pause at intervals, and his breathing was hard and painful; and even while thus resting he was in a position of terrible strain, and his pushing against the swing caused it to press hard against his windpipe and nearly strangle him.

After amazing effort he had elevated the lower end of his body until it protruded above the railing, the top of which was now across the lower end of his abdomen. Gradually he worked his body over, going backward, until there was sufficient excess of weight on the outer side of the rail; and then, with a quick lurch, he raised his head and shoulders and swung into a horizontal position on top of the rail. Of course, he would have fallen to the floor below had it not been for the line which he held in his teeth. With so great nicety had he estimated the distance between his mouth and the point where the rope was fastened to the rail, that the line tightened and checked him just as he reached the horizontal position on the rail. If one had told me beforehand that such a feat as I had just seen this man accomplish was possible, I should have thought him a fool.

Neranya was now balanced on his stomach across the top of the rail, and he eased his position by bending his spine and hanging down on either side as much as possible. Having rested thus for some minutes, he began cautiously to slide off backward, slowly paying out the line through is teeth, finding almost a fatal difficulty in passing the knots. Now, it is quite possible that the line would have escaped altogether from his teeth laterally when he would slightly relax his hold to let it slip, had it not been for a very ingenious plan to which he had resorted. This consisted in his having made a turn of the line around his neck before he attacked the wing, thus securing a threefold control of the line—one by his teeth, another by friction against his neck, and a third by his ability to compress it between his cheek and shoulder. It was quite evident now that the minutest details of a most elaborate plan had been carefully worked out by him before beginning the task, and that possibly weeks of difficult theoretical study had been consumed in mental preparation. As I observed him I was reminded of certain hitherto unaccountable things which he had been doing for some weeks past—going through certain hitherto inexplicable motions, undoubtedly for the purpose of training his muscles for the immeasurably arduous labor which he was now performing.

A stupendous and seemingly impossible part of his task had been accomplished. Could he reach the floor in safety? Gradually he worked himself backward over the rail, in imminent danger of falling; but his nerve never wavered, and I could see a wonderful light in his eyes. With something of a lurch, his body fell against the outer side of the railing, to which he was hanging by his chin, the line still held firmly in his teeth. Slowly he slipped his chin from the rail, and then hung suspended by the line in his teeth. By almost imperceptible degrees, with infinite caution, he descended the line, and, finally, his unwieldy body rolled upon the floor, safe and unhurt!

What miracle would this superhuman monster next accomplish? I was quick and strong, and was ready and able to intercept any dangerous act; but not until danger appeared would I interfere with this extraordinary scene.

I must confess to astonishment upon having observed that Neranya, instead of proceeding directly toward the sleeping rajah, took quite another direction. Then it was only escape, after all, that the wretch contemplated, and not the murder of the rajah. But how could he escape? The only possible way to reach the outer air without great risk was by ascending the stairs to the balcony and leaving by the corridor which opened upon it, and thus fall into the hands of some British soldiers quartered thereabout, who might conceive the idea of hiding him; but surely it was impossible for Neranya to ascend that long flight of stairs! Nevertheless, he made directly for them, his method of progression this: He lay upon his back, with the lower end of his body toward the stairs; then bowed his spine upward, thus drawing his head and shoulders a little forward; straightened, and then pushed the lower end of his body forward a space equal to that through which he had drawn his head; repeating this again and again, each time, while bending his spine preventing his head from slipping by pressing it against the floor. His progress was laborious and slow, but sensible; and, finally, he arrived at the foot of the stairs.

It was manifest that his insane purpose was to ascend them. The desire for freedom must have been strong within him! Wriggling to an upright position against the newel-post, he looked up at the great height which he had to climb, and sighed; but there was no dimming of the light in his eyes. How could he accomplish the impossible task?

His solution of the problem was very simple, though daring and perilous as all the rest. While leaning against the newel-post he let himself fall diagonally upon the bottom step, where he lay partly hanging over, but safe, on his side. Turning upon his back, he wriggled forward along the step to the rail and raised himself to an upright position against it as he had against the newl-post, fell as before, and landed on the second step. In this manner, with inconceivable labor, he accomplished the ascent of the entire flight of stairs.

It being apparent to me that the rajah was not the object of Neranya's movements, the anxiety which I had felt on that account was now entirely dissipated. The things which already he had accomplished were entirely beyond the nimblest imagination. The sympathy which I had always felt for the wretched man was now greatly quickened; and as infinitesimally small as I knew his chances for escape to be, I nevertheless hoped that he would succeed. Any assistance from me, however, was out of the question; and it never should be known that I had witnessed the escape.

Neranya was now upon the balcony, and I could dimly see him wriggling along toward the door which led out upon the balcony. Finally he stopped and wriggled to an upright position against the rail, which had wide openings between the balusters. His back was toward me, but he slowly turned and faced me and the hall. At the great distance I could not distinguish his features, but the slowness with which he had worked, even before he had fully accomplished the ascent of the stairs, was evidence all too eloquent of his extreme exhaustion. Nothing but a most desperate resolution could have sustained him thus far, but he had drawn upon the last remnant of his strength. He looked around the hall with a sweeping glance, and then down upon the rajah, who was sleeping immediately beneath him, over twenty feet below. He looked long and earnestly, sinking lower, and lower, and lower upon the rail. Suddenly, to my inconceivable astonishment and dismay, he toppled through and shot downward from his lofty height! I held my breath, expecting to see him crushed upon the stone floor beneath; but instead of that he fell full upon the rajah's breast, driving him through the cot to the floor. I sprang forward with a loud cry for help, and was instantly at the scene of the catastrophe. With indescribable horror I saw that Neranya's teeth were buried in the rajah's throat! I tore the wretch away, but the blood was pouring from the rajah's arteries, his chest was crushed in, and he was gasping in the agony of death. People came running in, terrified. I turned to

Neranya. He lay upon his back, his face hideously smeared with blood. Murder, and not escape, had been his intention from the beginning; and he had employed the only method by which there was ever a possibility of accomplishing it. I knelt beside him, and saw that he, too, was dying; his back had been broken by the fall. He smiled sweetly into my face, and a triumphant look of accomplished revenge sat upon his face even in death.

THE HORROR AT CHILTON CASTLE

JOSEPH PAYNE BRENNAN

I had decided to spend a leisurely summer in Europe, concentrating, if at all, on genealogical research. I went first to Ireland, journeying to Kilkenny, where I unearthed a mine of legend and authentic lore concerning my remote Irish ancestors, the O'Braonians, chiefs of Ui Duach in the ancient kingdom of Ossory. The Brennans (as the name was later spelled) lost their estates in the British confiscation under Thomas Wentworth, Earl of Strafford. The thieving Earl, I am happy to report, was subsequently beheaded in the Tower.

From Kilkenny I travelled to London and then to Chesterfield in search of maternal ancestors: the Holborns, Wilkersons, Searles, etc. Incomplete and fragmentary records left many great gaps, but my efforts were moderately successful and at length I decided to go farther north and visit the vicinity of Chilton Castle, seat of Robert Chilton-Payne, the twelfth Earl of Chilton. My relationship to the Chilton-Paynes was a most distant one, and yet there existed a tenuous thread of past connection and I thought it would amuse me to glimpse the castle.

Arriving in Wexwold, the tiny village near the castle, late in the afternoon, I engaged a room at the Inn of the Red Goose—the only one there was—unpacked and went down for a simple meal consisting of a small loaf, cheese and ale.

By the time I finished this stark and yet satisfying repast, darkness had set in, and with it came wind and rain.

I resigned myself to an evening at the inn. There was ale enough and I was in no hurry to go anywhere.

After writing a few letters, I went down and ordered a pint of ale. The taproom was almost deserted; the bartender, a stout gentleman who seemed forever on the point of falling asleep, was pleasant but taciturn, and at length I fell to musing on the strange and frightening legend of Chilton Castle.

There were variations of the legend, and without doubt the original tale had been embroidered down through the centuries, but the essential outline of the story concerned a secret room somewhere in the castle. It was said that this room contained a terrifying spectacle which the Chilton-Paynes were obliged to keep hidden from the world.

Only three persons were ever permitted to enter the room: the presiding Earl of Chilton, the Earl's male heir and one other person designated by the Earl. Ordinarily this person was the Factor of Chilton Castle. The room was entered only once in a generation; within three days after the male heir came of age, he was conducted to the secret room by the Earl and the Factor. The room was then sealed and never opened again until the heir conducted his own son to the grisly chamber.

According to the legend, the heir was never the same person again after entering the room. Invariably he would become somber and withdrawn; his countenance would acquire a brooding, apprehensive expression which nothing could long dispel. One of the earlier earls of Chilton had gone completely mad and hurled himself from the turrets of the castle.

Speculation about the contents of the secret room had continued for centuries. One version of the table described the panic-stricken flight of the Gowers, with armed enemies hot on their flagging heels. Although there had been bad blood between the Chilton-Paynes and the Gowers, in their desperation the Gowers begged for refuge at Chilton Castle. The Earl gave them entry, conducted them to a hidden room and left with a promise that they would be shielded from their pursuers. The Earl kept his promise; the Gowers' enemies were turned away from the Castle, their murderous plans unconsummated. The Earl, however, simply left the Gowers in the locked room to starve to death. The chamber was not opened until thirty years later, when the Earl's son finally broke the seal. A fearful sight met his eyes. The Gowers had starved to death slowly, and at the last, judging by the appearance of the mingled skeletons, had turned to cannibalism.

Another version of the legend indicated that the secret room had been used by medieval earls as a torture chamber. It was said that the ingenious instruments of pain were yet in the room and that these lethal apparatuses still clutched the pitiful remains of their final victims, twisted fearfully in their last agonies.

A third version mentioned one of the female ancestors of the Chilton-Paynes, Lady Susan Glanville, who had reputedly made a pact with the Devil. She had been condemned as a witch but had somehow managed to escape the stake. The date and even the manner of her death were unknown, but in some vague way the secret room was supposed to be connected with it.

As I speculated on these different versions of the gruesome legend, the storm increased in intensity. Rain drummed steadily against the leaded windows of the inn and now I could occasionally hear the distant mutter of thunder.

Glancing at the rain-streaked panes, I shrugged and ordered another pint of ale.

I had the fresh tankard halfway to my lips when the taproom door burst open, letting in a blast of wind and rain. The door was shut and a tall figure, muffled to the ears in a dripping greatcoat, moved to the bar. Removing his cap, he ordered brandy.

Having nothing better to do, I observed him closely. He looked about seventy, grizzled and weather-worn, but wiry, with an appearance of toughness and determination. He was frowning, as if absorbed in thinking through some unpleasant problem, yet his cold blue eyes inspected me keenly for a brief but deliberate interval.

I could not place him in a tidy niche. He might be a local farmer, and yet I did not think that he was. He had a vague aura of authority, and though his clothes were certainly plain, they were, I thought, somewhat better in cut and quality than those of the local countrymen I had observed.

A trivial incident opened a conversation between us. An unusually sharp crack of thunder made him turn towards the window. As he did so, he accidentally brushed his wet cap onto the floor. I retrieved it for him; he thanked me; and then we exchanged commonplace remarks about the weather.

I had an intuitive feeling that although he was normally a reticent individual, he was presently wrestling with some severe problem which made him want to hear a human voice. Realizing there was always the possibility that my intuition might, for once, have failed me, I nevertheless babbled on about my trip, about my genealogical researches in Kilkenny,

London and Chesterfield, and finally about my distant relationship to the Chilton-Paynes and my desire to get a good
look at Chilton Castle.

Suddenly I found that he was gazing at me with an
expression which, if not fierce, was disturbingly intense. An
awkward silence ensued. I coughed, wondering uneasily what I
had said to make those cold blue eyes stare at me so fixedly.

At length he became aware of my growing embarrassment.
"You must excuse me for staring," he apologized, "but
something you said . . . " He hesitated. "Could we perhaps take
that table?" He nodded towards a small table which sat half in
shadow in the far corner of the room.

I agreed, mystified but curious, and we took our drinks to
the secluded table.

He sat frowning for a minute, as if uncertain how to begin.
Finally he introduced himself as William Cowath. I gave him
my name and still he hesitated. At length he took a swallow of
brandy and then looked straight at me. "I am," he stated, "the
Factor at Chilton Castle."

I surveyed him with surprise and renewed interest. "What
an agreeable coincidence!" I exclaimed. "Then perhaps tomorrow you could arrange for me to have a look at the castle?"

He seemed scarcely to hear me. "Yes, yes, of course," he
replied absently.

Puzzled and a bit irritated by his air of detachment, I
remained silent.

He took a deep breath and then spoke rapidly, running
some of his words together. "Robert Chilton-Payne, the
Twelfth Earl of Chilton, was buried in the family vaults one
week ago. Frederick, the young heir and now Thirteenth Earl,
came of age just three days ago. Tonight it is imperative that he
be conducted to the secret chamber!"

I gaped at him in incredulous amazement. For a moment I

had an idea that he had somehow heard of my interest in Chilton Castle and was merely "pulling my leg" for amusement in the belief that I was the greenest of gullible tourists.

But there could be no mistaking his deadly seriousness. There was not the faintest suspicion of humor in his eyes.

I groped for words. "It seems so strange—so unbelievable! Just before you arrived, I had been thinking about the various legends connected with the secret room."

His cold eyes held my own. "It is not legend that confronts us; it is fact."

A thrill of fear and excitement ran through me. "You are going there—tonight?"

He nodded. "Tonight. Myself, the young Earl—and one other."

I stared at him.

"Ordinarily," he continued, "the Earl himself would accompany us. That is the custom. But he is dead. Shortly before he passed away, he instructed me to select someone to go with the young Earl and myself. That person must be male—and preferably of the blood."

I took a deep drink of ale and said not a word.

He continued. "Besides the young Earl, there is no one at the Castle save his elderly mother, Lady Beatrice Chilton, and an ailing aunt."

"Who could the Earl have had in mind?" I enquired cautiously.

The Factor frowned. "There are some distant male cousins residing in the country. I have an idea he thought at least one of them might appear for the obsequies. But not one of them did."

"That was most unfortunate!" I observed.

"Extremely unfortunate. And I am therefore asking you,

as one of the blood, to accompany the young Earl and myself to the secret room tonight!"

I gulped like a bumpkin. Lightning flashed against the windows and I could hear rain swishing along the stones outside. When feathers of ice stopped fluttering in my stomach, I managed a reply.

"But I . . . that is . . . my relationship is so very remote! I am 'of the blood' by courtesy only, you might say. The strain in me is so very diluted."

He shrugged. "You bear the name. And you possess at least a few drops of the Payne blood. Under the present urgent circumstances, no more is necessary. I am sure that the old Earl would agree with me, could he still speak. You will come?"

There was no escaping the intensity, the pressure, of those cold blue eyes. They seemed to follow my mind about as it groped for further excuses.

Finally, inevitably it seemed, I agreed. A feeling grew in me that the meeting had been preordained, that somehow I had always been destined to visit the secret chamber in Chilton Castle.

We finished our drinks and I went up to my room for rainwear. When I descended, suitably attired for the storm, the obese bartender was snoring on his stool, in spite of savage crashes of thunder, which had now become almost incessant. I envied him as I left the cozy room with William Cowath.

Once outside, my guide informed me that we would have to go on foot to the castle. He had purposely walked down to the inn, he explained, in order that he might have time and solitude to straighten out in his own mind the things which he would have to do.

The sheets of heavy rain, the strong wind and the roar of

thunder made conversation difficult. I walked Indian-fashion behind the Factor, who took enormous strides and appeared to know every inch of the way in spite of the darkness.

We walked only a short distance down the village street and then struck into a side road, which very soon dwindled to a footpath made slippery and treacherous by the driving rain.

Abruptly the path began to ascend; the footing became more precarious. It was at once necessary to concentrate all one's attention on one's feet. Fortunately, the flashes of lightning were frequent.

It seemed to me that we had been walking for an hour— actually, I suppose, it was only a few minutes—when the Factor finally stopped.

I found myself standing beside him on a flat, rocky plateau. He pointed up an incline which rose before us. "Chilton Castle," he said.

For a moment I saw nothing in the unrelieved darkness. Then the lightning flashed.

Beyond high battlemented walls, fissured with age, I glimpsed a great square Norman castle with four rectangular corner towers pierced by narrow window apertures which looked like evil slitted eyes. The huge, weathered pile was half-covered by a mantle of ivy which appeared more black than green.

"It looks incredibly old!" I commented.

William Cowath nodded. "It was begun in 1122 by Henry de Montargis." Without another word he started up the incline.

As we approached the castle wall, the storm grew worse. The slanting rain and powerful wind now made speech all but impossible. We bent our heads and staggered upwards.

When the wall finally loomed in front of us, I was amazed at its height and thickness. It had been constructed, obviously, to withstand the best siege guns and battering rams which its early enemies could bring to bear on it.

As we crossed a massive, timbered drawbridge, I peered down into the black ditch of a moat but I could not be sure whether there was water in it. A low, arched gateway gave access through the wall to an inner, cobblestoned courtyard. This courtyard was entirely empty, save for rivulets of rushing water.

Crossing the cobblestones with swift strides, the Factor led me to another arched gateway in yet another wall. Inside was a second, smaller yard and beyond spread the ivy-clutched base of the ancient keep itself.

Traversing a darkened, stone-flagged passage, we found ourselves facing a ponderous door, age-blackened oak reinforced with pitted bands of iron. The Factor flung open this door and there before us was the great hall of the castle.

Four long, hand-hewn tables with their accompanying benches stretched almost the entire length of the hall. Metal torch brackets, stained with age, were affixed to sculptured stone columns which supported the roof. Ranged around the walls were suits of armor, heraldic shields, halberds, pikes and banners—the accumulated trophies and prizes of bloody centuries when each castle was almost a kingdom unto itself. In flickering candlelight, which appeared to be the only illumination, the grim array was eerily impressive.

William Cowath waved a hand. "The holders of Chilton lived by the sword for many centuries."

Walking the length of the great hall, he entered another dim passageway. I followed silently.

As we strode along, he spoke in a subdued voice. "Frederick, the young heir, does not enjoy robust health. The shock of his father's death was severe—and he dreads tonight's ordeal, which he knows must come."

Stopping before a wooden door embellished with carved fleurs-de-lis and metal scrollwork, he gave me a shadowed, enigmatic glance and then knocked.

Someone enquired who was there and he identified himself. Presently a heavy bolt was lifted and the door opened.

If the Chilton-Paynes had been stubborn fighters in their day, the warrior blood appeared to have become considerably diluted in the veins of Frederick, the young heir and now Thirteenth Earl. I saw before me a thin, pale-complexioned young man whose dark sunken eyes looked haunted and fearful. His dress was both theatrical and anachronistic: a dark green velvet coat and trousers, a green satin waist-band, flounces of white lace at neck and wrists.

He beckoned us in as if with reluctance and closed the door. The walls of the small room were entirely covered with tapestries depicting the hunt or medieval battle scenes. A draught of air from a window or other aperture made them undulate constantly; they seemed to have a disturbing life of their own. In one corner of the room there was an antique canopy bed; in another a large writing-table with an agate lamp.

After a brief introduction, which included an explanation of how I came to be accompanying them, the Factor enquired if his Lordship was ready to visit the chamber.

Although he was wan in any case, Frederick's face now lost every last trace of color. He nodded, however, and preceded us into the passage.

William Cowath led the way; the young Earl followed him, and I brought up the rear.

At the far end of the passage, the Factor opened the door of a cobwebbed supply room. Here he secured candles, chisels, a pick and a sledgehammer. After packing these into a leather bag which he slung over one shoulder, he picked up a faggot torch which lay on one of the shelves in the room. He lit this, then waited while it flared into a steady flame. Satisfied with this illumination, he closed the room and beckoned for us to continue after him.

Nearby was a descending spiral of stone steps. Lifting his torch, the Factor started down. We trailed after him wordlessly.

There must have been fifty steps in that long, downward spiral. As we descended, the stones became wet and cold; the air, too, grew colder, but the cold was not of the type that refreshes. It was too laden with the smell of mold and dampness.

At the bottom of the steps we faced a tunnel, pitch-black and silent.

The Factor raised his torch. "Chilton Castle is Norman, but is said to have been reared over a Saxon ruin. It is believed that the passageways in these depths were constructed by the Saxons." He peered, frowning, into the tunnel. "Or by some still earlier folk."

He hesitated briefly, and I thought he was listening. Then, glancing round at us, he proceeded down the passage.

I walked after the Earl, shivering. The dead, icy air seemed to pierce to the pith of my bones. The stones underfoot grew slippery with a film of slime. I longed for more light, but there was none save that cast by the flickering, bobbing torch of the Factor.

Partway down the passage he paused, and again I sensed that he was listening. The silence seemed absolute, however, and we went on.

The end of the passage brought us to more descending steps. We went down some fifteen and entered another tunnel which appeared to have been cut out of the solid rock on which the castle had been reared. White-crusted nitre clung to the walls. The reek of mold was intense. The icy air was fetid with some other odor which I found peculiarly repellent, though I could not name it.

At last the Factor stopped, lifted his torch and slid the leather bag from his shoulder.

I saw that we stood before a wall made of some kind of building stone. Though damp and stained with nitre, it was obviously of much more recent construction than anything we had previously encountered.

Glancing round at us, William Cowath handed me the torch. "Keep a good hold on it, if you please. I have candles, but..."

Leaving the sentence unfinished, he drew the pick from his sling bag and began an assault on the wall. The barrier was solid enough but after he had worked a hole in it, he took up the sledgehammer and quicker progress was made. Once I offered to take up the hammer while he held the torch, but he only shook his head and went on with his work of demolition.

All this time the young Earl had not spoken a word. As I looked at his tense white face, I felt sorry for him, in spite of my own mounting trepidation.

Abruptly there was silence as the Factor lowered the sledgehammer. I saw that a good two feet of the lower wall remained.

William Cowath bent to inspect it. "Strong enough," he commented cryptically. "I will leave that to build on. We can step over it."

For a full minute he stood looking silently into the blackness beyond. Finally, shouldering his bag, he took the torch from my hand and stepped over the ragged base of the wall. We followed suit.

As I entered that chamber, the fetid odor which I had noticed in the passage seemed to overwhelm us. It washed around us in a nauseating wave and we all gasped for breath.

The Factor spoke between coughs. "It will subside in a minute or two. Stand near the aperture."

Although the reek remained repellently strong, we could at length breathe more freely.

William Cowath lifted his torch and peered into the black depths of the chamber. Fearfully, I gazed around his shoulder.

There was no sound and at first I could see nothing but nitre-encrusted walls and wet stone floor. Presently, however, in a far corner, just beyond the flickering halo of the faggot torch, I saw two tiny, fiery spots of red. I tried to convince myself that they were two red jewels, two rubies, shining in the torchlight.

But I knew at once—I *felt* at once—what they were. They were two red eyes and they were watching us with a fierce, unwavering stare.

The Factor spoke softly. "Wait here."

He crossed towards the corner, stopped halfway and held out his torch at arm's length. For a moment he was silent. Finally he emitted a long, shuddering sigh.

When he spoke again, his voice had changed. It was only a sepulchral whisper. "Come forward," he told us in that strange, hollow voice.

I followed Frederick until we stood at either side of the Factor.

When I saw what crouched on a stone bench in that far corner, I felt sure that I would faint. My heart literally stopped beating for perceptible seconds. The blood left my extremities; I reeled with dizziness. I might have cried out, but my throat would not open.

The entity which rested on that stone bench was like something that had crawled up out of hell. Piercing, malignant red eyes proclaimed that it had a terrible life, and yet that life sustained itself in a black, shrunken, half-mummified body which resembled a disinterred corpse. A few moldy rags clung to the cadaver-like frame. Wisps of white hair sprouted out of its ghastly gray-white skull. A red smear or blotch of some sort covered the wizened slit which served it as a mouth.

It surveyed us with a malignancy which was beyond anything merely human. It was impossible to stare back into those monstrous red eyes. They were so inexpressibly evil, one felt that one's soul would be consumed in the fires of their malevolence.

Glancing aside, I saw that the Factor was now supporting Frederick. The young heir had sagged against him, staring fixedly at the fearful apparition with terror-glazed eyes. In spite of my own sense of horror, I pitied him.

The Factor sighed again and then he spoke once more in that low, sepulchral voice.

"You see before you," he told us, "Lady Susan Glanville. She was carried into this chamber and chained to the wall in 1473."

A thrill of horror coursed through me; I felt that we were in the presence of malign forces from the Pit itself.

To me the hideous thing had appeared sexless, but at the sound of its name, the ghastly mockery of a grin contorted the puckered, red-smeared mouth.

I noticed now for the first time that the monster actually was secured to the wall. The great double shackles were so blackened with age, I had not noticed them before.

The Factor went on, as if he spoke by rote. "Lady Glanville was a maternal ancestor of the Chilton-Paynes. She had commerce with the Devil. She was condemned as a witch but escaped the stake. Finally her own people forcibly overcame her. She was brought in here, fettered and left to die."

He was silent a moment and then continued. "It was too late. She had already made a pact with the Powers of Darkness. It was an unspeakably evil thing and it has condemned her issue to a life of torment and nightmare, a lifetime of terror and dread."

He swung his torch towards the blackened, red-eyed thing. "She was a beauty once. She hated death. She feared death. And so she finally bartered her own immortal soul—and the bodies of her issue—for eternal earthly life."

I heard his voice as in a nightmare; it seemed to be coming from an infinite distance.

He went on. "The consequences of breaking the pact are too terrible to describe. No descendant of hers has ever dared to do so, once the forfeit is known. And so she has bided here for these nearly five hundred years."

I had thought he was finished, but he resumed. Glancing upwards, he lifted his torch towards the roof of that accursed chamber. "This room," he said, "lies directly underneath the family vaults. Upon the death of the Earl, the body is ostensibly left in the vaults. When the mourners have gone, however, the false bottom of the vault is thrust aside and the body of the Earl is lowered into this room."

Looking up, I saw the square rectangle of a trap-door above.

The Factor's voice now became barely audible. "Once every generation Lady Glanville feeds—on the corpse of the deceased Earl. It is a provision of that unspeakable pact which cannot be broken."

I knew now—with a sense of horror utterly beyond description—whence came that red smear on the repulsive mouth of the creature before us.

As if to confirm his words, the Factor lowered his torch

until its flame illuminated the floor at the foot of the stone bench where the vampiric monster was fettered.

Strewn about the floor were the scattered bones and skull of an adult male, red with fresh blood. And at some distance were other human bones, brown and crumbling with age.

At this point, Frederick began to scream. His shrill, hysterical cries filled the chamber. Although the Factor shook him roughly, his terrible shrieks continued, terror-filled, nerve-shaking.

For moments the corpse-like thing on the bench watched him with its frightful red eyes. It uttered sound finally, a kind of animal squeal which might have been intended as laughter.

Abruptly then, and without any warning, it slid from the bench and lunged towards the young Earl. The blackened shackles which fettered it to the wall permitted it to advance only a yard or two. It was pulled back sharply; yet it lunged again and again, squealing with a kind of hellish glee which stirred the hair on my head.

William Cowath thrust his torch towards the monster, but it continued to lunge at the end of its fetters. The nightmare room resounded with the Earl's screams and the creature's horrible squeals of bestial laughter. I felt that my own mind would give way unless I escaped from that anteroom of hell.

For the first time during an ordeal which would have sent any lesser man fleeing for his life and sanity, the iron control of the Factor appeared to be shaken. He looked beyond the wild lunging thing towards the wall where the fetters were fastened.

I sensed what was in his mind. Would those fastenings hold, after all these centuries of rust and dampness?

On a sudden resolve he reached into an inner pocket and drew out something which glittered in the torchlight. It was a silver crucifix. Striding forward, he thrust it almost into the twisted face of the leaping monstrosity which had once been the ravishing Lady Susan Glanville.

The creature reeled back with an agonized scream which drowned out the cries of the Earl. It cowered on the bench, abruptly silent and motionless, only the pulsating of its wizened mouth and the fires of hatred in its red eyes giving evidence that it still lived.

William Cowath addressed it grimly. "Creature of hell! If ye leave that bench 'ere we quit this room and seal it once again, I swear that I shall hold this cross against ye!"

The Thing's red eyes watched the Factor with an expression of abysmal hatred which no combination of mere letters could convey. They actually appeared to glow with fire. And yet I read in them something else—fear.

I suddenly became aware that silence had descended on that room of the damned. It lasted only a few moments. The Earl had finally stopped screaming, but now came something worse. He began to laugh.

It was only a low chuckle, but it was somehow worse than all his screams. It went on and on, softly, mindlessly.

The Factor turned, beckoning me towards the partially demolished wall. Crossing the room, I climbed out. Behind me the Factor led the young Earl, who shuffled like an old man, chuckling to himself.

There was then what seemed an interminable interval, during which the Factor carried back a sack of mortar and a keg of water which he had previously left somewhere in the tunnel. Working by torchlight, he prepared the cement and proceeded to seal up the chamber, using the same stones which he had displaced.

While the Factor labored, the young Earl sat motionless in the tunnel, chuckling softly.

There was silence from within. Once, only, I heard the Thing's fetters clank against the stone.

At last the Factor finished and led us back through those nitre-stained passageways and up the icy stairs. The Earl could scarcely ascend; with difficulty the Factor supported him from step to step.

Back in his tapestry-panelled chamber, Frederick sat on his canopy bed and stared at the floor, laughing quietly. With horror I noticed that his black hair had actually turned gray. After persuading him to drink a glass of liquid which I had no doubt contained a heavy dose of sedative, the Factor managed to get him stretched out on the bed.

William Cowath then led me to a nearby bedchamber. My impulse was to rush from that hellish pile without delay, but the storm still raged and I was by no means sure I could find my way back to the village without a guide.

The Factor shook his head sadly. "I fear his Lordship is doomed to an early death. He was never strong and tonight's events may have deranged his mind . . . may have weakened him beyond hope of recovery."

I expressed my sympathy and horror. The Factor's cold blue eyes held my own. "It may be," he said, "that in the event of the young Earl's death, you yourself might be considered . . ." He hesitated. "Might be considered," he finally concluded, "as one somewhat in the line of succession."

I wanted to hear no more. I gave him a curt goodnight, bolted the door after him and tried—quite unsuccessfully—to salvage a few minutes' sleep.

But sleep would not come. I had feverish visions of that red-eyed thing in the sealed chamber escaping its fetters, breaking through the wall and crawling up those icy, slime-covered stairs. . . .

Even before dawn I softly unbolted my door and, like a marauding thief, crept shivering through the cold passageways and the great hall of the castle. Crossing the cobbled courtyards and the black moat, I scrambled down the incline towards the village.

Long before noon I was well on my way to London. Luck was with me; the next day I was on a boat bound for the Atlantic run.

I shall never return to England. I intend always to keep Chilton Castle and its permanent occupant at least an ocean away.

A CASE OF EAVESDROPPING

ALGERNON BLACKWOOD

Jim Shorthouse was the sort of fellow who always made a mess of things. Everything with which his hands or mind came into contact issued from such contact in an unqualified and irremediable state of mess. His college days were a mess: he was twice rusticated. His schooldays were a mess: he went to half a dozen, each passing him to the next with a worse character and in a more developed state of mess. His early boyhood was the sort of mess that copy-books and dictionaries spell with a big "M," and his babyhood—ugh! was the embodiment of howling, yowling, screaming mess.

At the age of forty, however, there came a change in his troubled life, when he met a girl with half a million in her own right, who consented to marry him, and who very soon succeeded in raising his most messy existence into a state of comparative order and system.

Certain incidents, important and otherwise, of Jim's life would never have come to be told here but for the fact that in getting into his "messes" and out of them again he succeeded in drawing himself into the atmosphere of peculiar circumstances and strange happenings. He attracted to his path the curious adventures of life as unfailingly as meat attracts flies, and jam wasps. It is to the meat and jam of his life, so to speak, that he owes his experiences; his after-life was all pudding, which attracts nothing but greedy children. With marriage the interest of life ceased for all but one person, and his path became regular as the sun's instead of erratic as a comet's.

The first experience in order of time that he related to me shows that somewhere latent behind his disarranged nervous system there lay psychic perceptions of an uncommon order. About the age of twenty-two—I think after his second rustication—his father's purse and patience had equally given out, and Jim found himself stranded high and dry in a large American city. High and dry! And the only clothes that had no holes in them safely in the keeping of his uncle's wardrobe.

Careful reflection on a bench in one of the city parks led him to the conclusion that the only thing to do was to persuade the city editor of one of the daily journals that he possessed an observant mind and a ready pen, and that he could "do good work for your paper, sir, as a reporter." This, then, he did, standing at a most unnatural angle between the editor and the window to conceal the whereabouts of the holes.

"Guess we'll have to give you a week's trial," said the editor, who, ever on the lookout for good chance material, took on shoals of men in that way and retained on the average one man per shoal. Anyhow it gave Jim Shorthouse the wherewithal to sew up the holes and relieve his uncle's wardrobe of its burden.

Then he went to find living quarters; and in this proceeding his unique characteristics already referred to—what theosophists would call his Karma—began unmistakably to assert themselves, for it was in the house he eventually selected that this sad tale took place.

There are no "diggings" in American cities. The alternative for small incomes are grim enough—rooms in a boarding-house where meals are served, or in a rooming-house where no meals are served—not even breakfast. Rich people live in palaces, of course, but Jim had nothing to do with "sich-like." His horizon was bounded by boardinghouses and rooming houses; and owing to the necessary irregularity of his meals and hours, he took the latter.

It was a large, gaunt-looking place in a side street, with dirty windows and a creaking iron gate, but the rooms were large, and the one he selected and paid for in advance was on the top floor. The landlady looked gaunt and dusty as the house, and quite as old. Her eyes were green and faded, and her features large.

"Waal," she twanged, with her electrifying Western drawl, "that's the room, if you like it, and that's the price I said. Now, if you want it, why, just say so; and if you don't, why, it don't hurt me any."

Jim wanted to shake her, but he feared the clouds of long-accumulated dust in her clothes, and as the price and size of the room suited him, he decided to take it.

"Anyone else on this floor?" he asked.

She looked at him queerly out of her faded eyes.

"None of my guests ever put such questions to me before," she said, "but I guess you're different. Why, there's no one at all but an old gent that's stayed here every bit of five years. He's over thar," pointing to the end of the passage.

"Ah! I see," said Shorthouse feebly. "So I'm alone up here?"

"Reckon you are, pretty near," she twanged out, ending the conversation abruptly by turning her back on her new "guest" and going slowly and deliberately downstairs.

The newspaper work kept Shorthouse out most of the night. Three times a week he got home at 1 a.m., and three times at 3 a.m. The room proved comfortable enough, and he paid for a second week. His unusual hours had so far prevented his meeting any inmates of the house, and not a sound had been heard from the "old gent" who shared the floor with him. It seemed a very quiet house.

One night, about the middle of the second week, he came home tired after a long day's work. The lamp that usually stood all night in the hall had burned itself out, and he had to stumble upstairs in the dark. He made considerable noise in doing so, but nobody seemed to be disturbed. The whole house was utterly quiet, and probably everybody was asleep. There were no lights under any of the doors. All was in darkness. It was after two o'clock.

After reading some English letters that had come during the day, and dipping for a few minutes into a book, he became drowsy and got ready for bed. Just as he was about to get in between the sheets, he stopped for a moment and listened. There rose in the night, as he did so, the sound of steps somewhere in the house below. Listening attentively, he heard that it was somebody coming upstairs—a heavy tread, and the owner taking no pains to step quietly. On it came up the stairs, tramp, tramp, tramp—evidently the tread of a big man, and one in something of a hurry.

At once thoughts connected somewhere with fire and

police flashed through Jim's brain, but there were no sounds of voices with the steps, and he reflected in the same moment that it could only be the old gentleman keeping late hours and tumbling upstairs in the darkness. He was in the act of turning out the gas and stepping into bed, when the house resumed its former stillness by the footsteps suddenly coming to a dead stop immediately outside his own room.

With his hand on the gas, Shorthouse paused a moment before turning it out to see if the steps would go on again, when he was startled by a loud knocking on his door. Instantly, in obedience to a curious and unexplained instinct, he turned out the light, leaving himself and the room in total darkness.

He had scarcely taken a step across the room to open the door, when a voice from the other side of the wall, so close it almost sounded in his ear, exclaimed in German, "Is that you, Father? Come in."

The speaker was a man in the next room, and the knocking, after all, had not been on his own door, but on that of the adjoining chamber, which he had supposed to be vacant.

Almost before the man in the passage had time to answer in German, "Let me in at once," Jim heard someone cross the floor and unlock the door. Then it was slammed to with a bang, and there was audible the sound of footsteps about the room, and of chairs being drawn up to a table and knocking against furniture on the way. The men seemed wholly regardless of their neighbor's comfort, for they made noise enough to waken the dead.

"Serves me right for taking a room in such a cheap hole," reflected Jim in the darkness. "I wonder whom she's let the room to!"

The two rooms, the landlady had told him, were originally one. She had put up a thin partition—just a row of boards—to increase her income. The doors were adjacent, and only separated by the massive upright beam between them. When one was opened or shut the other rattled.

With utter indifference to the comfort of the other sleepers in the house, the two Germans had meanwhile commenced to talk both at once and at the top of their voices. They talked emphatically, even angrily. The words "Father" and "Otto" were freely used. Shorthouse understood German, but as he stood listening for the first minute or two, an eavesdropper in spite of himself, it was difficult to make head or tail of the talk, for neither would give way to the other, and the jumble of guttural sounds and unfinished sentences was wholly unintelligible. Then very suddenly, both voices dropped together; and, after a moment's pause, the deep tones of one of them, who seemed to be the "father," said, with the utmost distinctness—

"You mean, Otto, that you refuse to get it?"

There was a sound of someone shuffling in the chair before the answer came. "I mean that I don't know *how* to get it. It is so much, Father. It is *too* much. A part of it—"

"A part of it!" cried the other, with an angry oath, "a part of it, when ruin and disgrace are already in the house, is worse than useless. If you can get half you can get all, you wretched fool! Half-measures only damn all concerned."

"You told me last time—" began the other firmly, but was not allowed to finish. A succession of horrible oaths drowned his sentence, and the father went on, in a voice vibrating with anger—

"You know she will give you anything. You have only been married a few months. If you ask and give a plausible reason you can get all we want and more. You can ask it temporarily. All will be paid back. It will re-establish the firm, and she will never know what was done with it. With that amount, Otto, you know I can recoup all these terrible losses, and in less than a year all will be repaid. But without it . . . You must get it, Otto. Hear me, you must. Am I to be arrested for the misuse of trust moneys? Is our honored name to be cursed and spat on?" The old man choked and stammered in his anger and desperation.

Shorthouse stood shivering in the darkness and listening in spite of himself. The conversation had carried him along with it, and he had been for some reason afraid to let his neighborhood be known. But at this point he realized that he had listened too long and that he must inform the two men that they could be overheard to every single syllable. So he coughed loudly, and at the same time rattled the handle of his door. It seemed to have no effect, for the voices continued just as loudly as before, the son protesting and the father growing more and more angry. He coughed again persistently, and also contrived purposely in the darkness to tumble against the partition, feeling the thin boards yield easily under his weight, and making a considerable noise in so doing. But the voices went on unconcernedly, and louder than ever. Could it be possible they had not heard?

By this time Jim was more concerned about his own sleep than the morality of overhearing the private scandals of his neighbors, and he went out into the passage and knocked smartly at their door. Instantly, as if by magic, the sounds ceased. Everything dropped into utter silence. There was no light under the door and not a whisper could be heard within. He knocked again, but received no answer.

"Gentlemen," he began at length, with his lips close to the keyhole and in German, "please do not talk so loud. I can overhear all you say in the next room. Besides, it is very late, and I wish to sleep."

He paused and listened, but no answer was forthcoming. He turned the handle and found the door was locked. Not a sound broke the stillness of the night except the faint swish of the wind over the skylight and the creaking of a board here and there in the house below. The cold air of a very early morning crept down the passage, and made him shiver. The silence of the house began to impress him disagreeably. He looked behind him and about him, hoping, and yet fearing, that something would break the stillness. The voices still seemed to ring on in his ears; but that sudden silence, when he knocked at the door affected him far more unpleasantly than the voices, and put strange thoughts in his brain—thoughts he did not like or approve.

Moving stealthily from the door, he peered over the banisters into the space below. It was like a deep vault that might conceal in its shadows anything that was not good. It was not difficult to fancy he saw an indistinct moving to-and-fro below him. Was that a figure sitting on the stairs peering up obliquely at him out of hideous eyes? Was that a sound of whispering and shuffling down there in the dark halls and forsaken landings? Was it something more than the inarticulate murmur of the night?

The wind made an effort overhead, singing over the skylight, and the door behind him rattled and made him start. He turned to go back to his room, and the draft closed the door slowly in his face as if there were someone pressing against it from the other side. When he pushed it open and went in, a hundred shadowy forms seemed to dart swiftly and silently back to their corners and hiding-places. But in the adjoining room the sounds had entirely ceased, and Shorthouse soon crept into bed, and left the house with its inmates, waking or sleeping, to take care of themselves, while he entered the region of dreams and silence.

Next day, strong in the common sense that the sunlight brings, he determined to lodge a complaint against the noisy occupants of the next room and make the landlady request them to modify their voices at such late hours of the night and early morning. But it so happened that she was not to be seen that day, and when he returned from the office at midnight it was, of course, too late.

Looking under the door as he came up to bed he noticed that there was no light, and concluded that the Germans were not in. So much the better. He went to sleep about one o'clock, fully decided that if they came up later and woke him with their horrible noises he would not rest till he had roused the landlady and made her reprove them with that authoritative twang, in which every word was like the lash of a metallic whip.

However, there proved to be no need for such drastic measures, for Shorthouse slumbered peacefully all night, and his dreams—chiefly of the fields of grain and flocks of sheep on the faraway farms of his father's estate—were permitted to run their fanciful course unbroken.

Two nights later, however, when he came home tired out, after a difficult day, and wet and blown about by one of the wickedest storms he had ever seen, his dreams—always of the fields and sheep—were not destined to be so undisturbed.

He had already dozed off in that delicious glow that follows the removal of wet clothes and the immediate snuggling under warm blankets, when his consciousness, hovering on the borderland between sleep and waking, was vaguely troubled by a sound that rose indistinctly from the depths of the house, and, between the gusts of wind and rain, reached his ears with an accompanying sense of uneasiness and discomfort. It rose on the night air with some pretence of regularity, dying away again in the roar of the wind to reassert itself distantly in the deep, brief hushes of the storm.

For a few minutes Jim's dreams were colored only—tinged, as it were—by this impression of fear approaching from somewhere insensibly upon him. His consciousness, at first, refused to be drawn back from that enchanted region where it had wandered, and he did not immediately awaken. But the nature of his dreams changed unpleasantly. He saw the sheep suddenly run huddled together, as though frightened by the neighborhood of an enemy, while the fields of waving corn became agitated as though some monster were moving uncouthly among the crowded stalks. The sky grew dark, and in his dream an awful sound came somewhere from the clouds. It was in reality the sound downstairs growing more distinct.

Shorthouse shifted uneasily across the bed with something like a groan of distress. The next minute he awoke, and found himself sitting straight up in bed—listening. Was it a nightmare? Had he been dreaming evil dreams, that his flesh crawled and the hair stirred on his head?

The room was dark and silent, but outside the wind howled dismally and drove the rain with repeated assaults against the rattling windows. How nice it would be—the thought flashed through his mind—if all winds, like the west wind, went down with the sun! They made such fiendish noises at night, like the crying of angry voices. In the daytime they had such a different sound. If only—

Hark! It was no dream after all, for the sound was momentarily growing louder, and its *cause* was coming up the stairs. He found himself speculating feebly what this cause might be, but the sound was still too indistinct to enable him to arrive at any definite conclusion.

The voice of a church clock striking two made itself heard above the wind. It was just about the hour when the Germans had commenced their performance three nights before. Shorthouse made up his mind that if they began it again he would not put up with it for very long. Yet he was already horribly conscious of the difficulty he would have of getting out of bed. The clothes were so warm and comforting against his back. The sound, still steadily coming nearer, had by this time become differentiated from the confused clamor of the elements, and had resolved itself into the footsteps of one or more persons.

"The Germans, hang 'em!" thought Jim. "But what on earth is the matter with me? I never felt so queer in all my life."

He was trembling all over, and felt as cold as though he were in a freezing atmosphere. His nerves were steady enough but he was conscious of a curious sense of malaise and trepidation, such as even the most vigorous men have been known to experience when in the first grip of some horrible and deadly disease. As the footsteps approached, this feeling of weakness increased. He felt a strange lassitude creeping over him, a sort of exhaustion, accompanied by a growing numbness in the extremities, and a sensation of dreaminess in the head, as if perhaps the consciousness were leaving its accustomed seat in the brain and preparing to act on another plane. Yet, strange to say, as the vitality was slowly withdrawn from his body, his senses seemed to grow more acute.

Meanwhile the steps were already on the landing at the top of the stairs, and Shorthouse, still sitting upright in bed, heard a heavy body brush past his door and along the wall outside, almost immediately afterwards the loud knocking of someone's knuckles on the door of the adjoining room.

Instantly, though so far not a sound had proceeded from within, he heard, through the thin partition, a chair pushed back and a man quickly cross the floor and open the door.

"Ah! it's you," he heard in the son's voice. Had the fellow, then, been sitting silently in there all this time, waiting for his father's arrival? To Shorthouse it came not as a pleasant reflection by any means.

There was no answer to this dubious greeting, but the door was closed quickly, and then there was a sound as if a bag or parcel had been thrown on a wooden table and had slid some distance across it before stopping.

"What's that?" asked the son, with anxiety in his tone.

"You may know before I go," returned the other gruffly. Indeed his voice was more than gruff: it betrayed ill-suppressed passion.

Shorthouse was conscious of a strong desire to stop the conversation before it proceeded any further, but somehow or other his will was not equal to the task, and he could not get out of bed. The conversation went on, every tone and inflection distinctly audible above the noise of the storm.

In a low voice the father continued. Jim missed some of the words at the beginning of the sentence. It ended with: "... but now they've all left, and I've managed to get up to you. You know what I've come for." There was distinct menace in his tone.

"Yes," returned the other, "I have been waiting."

"And the money?" asked the father impatiently.

No answer.

"You've had three days to get it in, and I've contrived to stave off the worst so far—but tomorrow is the end."

No answer.

"Speak, Otto! What have you got for me? Speak, my son; for God's sake, tell me."

There was a moment's silence, during which the old man's vibrating accents seemed to echo through the rooms. Then came in a low voice the answer—

"I have nothing."

"Otto!" cried the other with passion, "nothing!"

"I can get nothing," came almost in a whisper.

"You lie!" cried the other, in a half-stifled voice. "I swear you lie. Give me the money."

A chair was heard scraping along the floor. Evidently the men had been sitting over the table, and one of them had risen. Shorthouse heard the bag or parcel drawn across the table, and then a step as if one of the men was crossing to the door.

"Father, what's in that? I must know," said Otto, with the first signs of determination in his voice. There must have been an effort on the son's part to gain possession of the parcel in question, and on the father's to retain it, for between them it fell to the ground. A curious rattle followed its contact with the floor. Instantly there were sounds of a scuffle. The men were struggling for the possession of the box. The elder man with oaths, and blasphemous imprecations, the other, with short gasps that betokened the strength of his efforts. It was of short duration, and the younger man had evidently won, for a minute later was heard his angry exclamation.

"I knew it. Her jewels! You scoundrel, you shall never have them. It is a crime."

The elder man uttered a short, guttural laugh, which froze Jim's blood and made his skin creep. No word was spoken, and for the space of ten seconds there was a living silence. Then the air trembled with the sound of a thud, followed immediately by a groan and the crash of a heavy body falling over onto the table. A second later there was a lurching from the table onto the floor and against the partition that separated the rooms. The bed quivered an instant at the shock, but the unholy spell was lifted from his soul and Jim Shorthouse sprang out of bed and across the floor in a single bound. He knew that ghastly murder had been done—the murder by a father of his son.

With shaking fingers but a determined heart he lit the gas,

and the first thing in which his eyes corroborated the evidence of his ears was the horrifying detail that the lower portion of the partition bulged unnaturally into his own room. The glaring paper with which it was covered had cracked under the tension and the boards beneath it bent inwards towards him. What hideous load was behind them, he shuddered to think.

All this he saw in less than a second. Since the final lurch against the wall not a sound had proceeded from the room, not even a groan or a footstep. All was still but the howl of the wind, which to his ears had in it a note of triumphant horror.

Shorthouse was in the act of leaving the room to rouse the house and send for the police—in fact his hand was already on the doorknob—when something in the room arrested his attention. Out of the corner of his eyes he thought he caught sight of something moving. He was sure of it, and turning his eyes in the direction, he found he was not mistaken.

Something was creeping slowly towards him along the floor. It was something dark and serpentine in shape, and it came from the place where the partition bulged. He stooped down to examine it with feelings of intense horror and repugnance, and he discovered that it was moving towards him from the *other side* of the wall. His eyes were fascinated, and for the moment he was unable to move. Silently, slowly, from side to side like a thick worm, it crawled forwards into the room beneath his frightened eyes, until at length he could stand it no longer and stretched out his arm to touch it. But at the instant of contact he withdrew his hand with a suppressed scream. It was sluggish—and it was warm! and he saw that his fingers were stained with living crimson.

A second more, and Shorthouse was out in the passage with his hand on the door of the next room. It was locked. He plunged forward with all his weight against it, and, the lock giving way, he fell headlong into a room that was pitch-dark and very cold. In a moment he was on his feet again and trying to penetrate the blackness. Not a sound, not a movement. Not even the sense of a presence. It was empty, miserably empty!

Across the room he could trace the outline of a window with rain streaming down the outside, and the blurred lights of the city beyond. But the room was empty, appallingly empty; and so still. He stood there, cold as ice, staring, shivering, listening. Suddenly there was a step behind him and a light flashed into the room, and when he turned quickly with his arm up as if to ward off a terrific blow he found himself face to face with the landlady. Instantly the reaction began to set in.

It was nearly three o'clock in the morning, and he was standing there with bare feet and striped pajamas in a small room, which in the merciful light he perceived to be absolutely empty, carpetless, and without a stick of furniture, or even a window blind. There he stood staring at the disagreeable landlady. And there she stood too, staring and silent, in a black wrapper, her head almost bald, her face white as chalk, shading a sputtering candle with one bony hand and peering over it at him with her blinking eyes. She looked positively hideous.

"Waal?" she drawled at length, "I heard yer right enough. Guess you couldn't sleep! Or just prowlin' round a bit—is that it?"

The empty room, the absence of all traces of the recent tragedy, the silence, the hour, his striped pajamas and bare feet—everything together combined to deprive him momentarily of speech. He stared at her blankly without a word.

"Waal?" clanked the awful voice.

"My dear woman," he burst out finally, "there's been something awful—" So far his desperation took him, but no further. He positively stuck at the substantive.

"Oh! there hasn't been nothin'," she said slowly still peering at him. "I reckon you've only seen and heard what the others did. I never can keep folks on this floor long. Most of 'em catch on sooner or later—that is, the ones that's kind of quick and sensitive. Only you being an Englishman I thought you wouldn't mind. Nothin' really happens; it's only thinkin' like."

Shorthouse was beside himself. He felt ready to pick her up and drop her over the banisters, candle and all.

"Look there," he said, pointing at her within an inch of her blinking eyes with the fingers that had touched the oozing blood; "look there, my good woman. Is that only thinking?"

She stared a minute, as if not knowing what he meant.

"I guess so," she said at length.

He followed her eyes, and to his amazement saw that his fingers were as white as usual, and quite free from the awful stain that had been there ten minutes before. There was no sign of blood. No amount of staring could bring it back. Had he gone out of his mind? Had his eyes and ears played such tricks with him? Had his senses become false and perverted? He dashed past the landlady, out into the passage, and gained his own room in a couple of strides. Whew! ... the partition no longer bulged. The paper was not torn. There was no creeping, crawling thing on the faded old carpet.

"It's all over now," drawled the metallic voice behind him. "I'm going to bed again."

He turned and saw the landlady slowly going downstairs again, still shading the candle with her hand and peering up at him from time to time as she moved. A black, ugly, unwholesome object, he thought, as she disappeared into the darkness below, and the last flicker of her candle threw a queer-shaped shadow along the wall and over the ceiling.

Without hesitating a moment, Shorthouse threw himself into his clothes and went out of the house. He preferred the storm to the horrors of that top floor, and he walked the streets till daylight.

In the evening he told the landlady he would leave the next day, in spite of her assurances that nothing more would happen.

"It never comes back," she said—"that is, not after he's killed."

Shorthouse gasped.

"You gave me a lot for my money," he growled.

"Waal, it aren't my show," she drawled. "I'm no spirit medium. You take chances. Some'll sleep right along and never hear nothin'. Others, like yourself, are different and get the whole thing."

"Who's the old gentleman?—does he hear it?" asked Jim.

"There's no old gentleman at all," she answered coolly. "I just told you that to make you feel easy like in case you did hear anythin'. You were all alone on the floor."

"Say now," she went on, after a pause in which Short-house could think of nothing to say but unpublishable things, "say now, do tell, did you feel sort of cold when the show was on, sort of tired and weak, I mean, as if you might be going to die?"

"How can I say?" he answered savagely. "What I felt God only knows."

"Waal, but He won't tell," she drawled out. "Only I was wonderin' how you really did feel, because the man who had that room last was found one morning in bed—"

"In bed?"

"He was dead. He was the one before you. Oh! You don't need to get rattled so. *You're* all right. And it all really happened, they do say. This house used to be a private residence some twenty-five years ago, and a German family of the name of Steinhardt lived here. They had a big business in Wall Street, and stood way up in things."

"Ah!" said her listener.

"Oh yes, they did, right at the top, till one fine day it all bust and the old man skipped with the boodle—"

"Skipped with the boodle?"

"That's so," she said. "Got clear away with all the money, and the son was found dead in his house, committed suicide it was thought. Though there was some as said he couldn't have stabbed himself and fallen in that position. They said he was murdered. The father died in prison. They tried to fasten the murder on him, but there was no motive, or no evidence, or no somethin'. I forget now."

"Very pretty," said Shorthouse.

"I'll show you somethin' mighty queer anyways," she drawled, "if you'll come upstairs a minute. I've heard the steps and voices lots of times; they don't phase me any. I'd just as lief hear so many dogs barkin'. You'll find the whole story in the newspapers if you look it up—not what goes on here, but the story of the Germans. My house would be ruined if they told all, and I'd sue for damages."

They reached the bedroom, and the woman went in and pulled up the edge of the carpet where Shorthouse had seen the blood soaking in the previous night.

"Look thar, if you feel like it," said the old hag. Stooping down, he saw a dark, dull stain in the boards that corresponded exactly to the shape and position of the blood as he had seen it.

That night he slept in a hotel, and the following day sought new quarters. In the newspapers on file in his office after a long search he found twenty years back the detailed story, substantially as the woman had said, of Steinhardt & Co.'s failure, the absconding and subsequent arrest of the senior partner, and the suicide, or murder, of the son Otto. The landlady's rooming house had formerly been their private residence.

LEININGEN VERSUS THE ANTS

CARL STEPHENSON

"Unless they alter their course, and there's no reason why they should, they'll reach your plantation in two days at the latest."

Leiningen sucked placidly at a cigar about the size of a corn cob and for a few seconds gazed without answering at the agitated District Commissioner. Then he took the cigar from his lips and leaned slightly forward. With his bristling grey hair, bulky nose, and lucid eyes, he had the look of an aging and shabby eagle.

"Decent of you," he murmured, "paddling all this way just to give me the tip. But you're pulling my leg, of course, when you say I must do a bunk. Why, even a herd of saurians couldn't drive me from this plantation of mine."

The Brazilian official threw up lean and lanky arms and clawed the air with wildly distended fingers. "Leiningen!" he shouted, "you're insane! They're not creatures you can fight—they're an elemental—an 'act of God!' Ten miles long, two miles wide—ants, nothing but ants! And every single one of them a fiend from hell; before you can spit three times they'll eat a full-grown buffalo to the bones. I tell you if you don't clear out at once there'll be nothing left of you but a skeleton picked as clean as your own plantation."

Leiningen grinned. "Act of God, my eye! Anyway, I'm not an old woman; I'm not going to run for it just because an elemental's on the way. And don't think I'm the kind of fathead who tries to fend off lightning with his fists, either. I use my intelligence, old man. With me, the brain isn't a second blind gut; I know what it's there for. When I began this model farm and plantation three years ago, I took into account all that could conceivably happen to it. And now I'm ready for anything and everything—including your ants."

The Brazilian rose heavily to his feet. "I've done my best," he gasped. "Your obstinacy endangers not only yourself, but the lives of your four hundred workers. You don't know these ants!"

Leiningen accompanied him down to the river, where the Government launch was moored. The vessel cast off. As it moved downstream, the exclamation mark neared the rail and began waving its arms frantically. Long after the launch had disappeared around the bend, Leiningen thought he could still hear that dimming, imploring voice. "You don't know them, I tell you! *You don't know them!*"

But the reported enemy was by no means unfamiliar to the planter. Before he started work on his settlement, he had lived long enough in the country to see for himself the fearful devastations sometimes wrought by these ravenous insects in their campaigns for food. But since then he had planned measures of defence accordingly, and these, he was convinced, were in every way adequate to withstand the approaching peril.

Moreover, during his three years as planter, Leiningen

had met and defeated drought, flood, plague, and all other "acts of God" which had come against him—unlike his fellow-settlers in the district, who had made little or no resistance. This unbroken success he attributed solely to the observance of his lifelong motto: *The human brain needs only to become fully aware of its powers to conquer even the elements.* Dullards reeled senselessly and aimlessly into the abyss; cranks, however brilliant, lost their heads when circumstances suddenly altered or accelerated and ran into stone walls; sluggards drifted with the current until they were caught in whirlpools and dragged under. But such disasters, Leiningen contended, merely strengthened his argument that intelligence, directed aright, invariably makes man the master of his fate.

Yes, Leiningen had always known how to grapple with life. Even here, in this Brazilian wilderness, his brain had triumphed over every difficulty and danger it had so far encountered. First he had vanquished primal forces by cunning and organization, then he had enlisted the resources of modern science to increase miraculously the yield of his plantation. And now he was sure he would prove more than a match for the "irresistible" ants.

That same evening, however, Leiningen assembled his workers. He had no intention of waiting till the news reached their ears from other sources. Most of them had been born in the district; the cry "The ants are coming!" was to them an imperative signal for instant, panic-stricken flight, a spring for life itself. But so great was the Indians' trust in Leiningen, in Leiningen's word, and in Leiningen's wisdom, that they received his curt tidings, and his orders for the imminent struggle, with the calmness with which they were given. They waited, unafraid, alert, as if for the beginning of a new game or hunt which he had just described to them. The ants were indeed mighty, but not so mighty as the boss. Let them come!

They came at noon the second day. Their approach was announced by the wild unrest of the horses, scarcely controllable now either in stall or under rider, scenting from afar a vapour instinct with horror.

It was announced by a stampede of animals, timid and savage, hurtling past each other; jaguars and pumas flashing by nimble stags of the pampas; bulky tapirs, no longer hunters, themselves hunted, outpacing fleet kinkajous; maddened herds of cattle, heads lowered, nostrils snorting, rushing through tribes of loping monkeys, chattering in a dementia of terror; then followed the creeping and springing denizens of bush and steppe, big and little rodents, snakes, and lizards.

Pell-mell the rabble swarmed down the hill to the plantation, scattered right and left before the barrier of the water-filled ditch, then sped onwards to the river, where, again hindered, they fled along its banks out of sight.

This water-filled ditch was one of the defence measures which Leiningen had long since prepared against the advent of the ants. It encompassed three sides of the plantation like a huge horseshoe. Twelve feet across, but not very deep, when dry it could hardly be described as an obstacle to either man or beast. But the ends of the "horseshoe" ran into the river which formed the northern boundary, and fourth side, of the plantation. And at the end nearer the house and outbuildings in the middle of the plantation, Leiningen had constructed a dam by means of which water from the river could be diverted into the ditch.

So now, by opening the dam, he was able to fling an imposing girdle of water, a huge quadrilateral with the river as its base, completely around the plantation, like the moat encircling a medieval city. Unless the ants were clever enough to build rafts, they had no hope of reaching the plantation, Leiningen concluded.

The twelve-foot water ditch seemed to afford in itself all the security needed. But while awaiting the arrival of the ants, Leiningen made a further improvement. The western section of the ditch ran along the edge of a tamarind wood, and the branches of some great trees reached over the water. Leiningen now had them lopped so that ants could not descend from them within the "moat."

The women and children, then the herds of cattle, were escorted by peons on rafts over the river, to remain on the other side in absolute safety until the plunderers had departed. Leiningen gave this instruction, not because he believed the non-combatants were in any danger, but in order to avoid hampering the efficiency of the defenders. "Critical situations first become crises," he explained to his men, "when oxen or women get excited."

Finally, he made a careful inspection of the "inner moat"—a smaller ditch lined with concrete, which extended around the hill on which stood the ranch house, barns, stables, and other buildings. Into this concrete ditch emptied the inflow pipes from three great petrol tanks. If by some miracle the ants managed to cross the water and reach the plantation this "rampart of petrol" would be an absolutely impassable protection for the besieged and their dwellings and stock. Such, at least, was Leiningen's opinion.

He stationed his men at irregular distances along the water ditch, the first line of defence. Then he lay down in his hammock and puffed drowsily away at his pipe until a peon came with the report that the ants had been observed far away in the south.

Leiningen mounted his horse, which at the feel of its master seemed to forget its uneasiness, and rode leisurely in the direction of the threatening offensive. The southern stretch of ditch—the upper side of the quadrilateral—was nearly three

...nes long; from its centre one could survey the entire countryside. This was destined to be the scene of the outbreak of war between Leiningen's brain and twenty square miles of life-destroying ants.

It was a sight one could never forget. Over the range of hills, as far as eye could see, crept a darkening hem, ever longer and broader, until the shadow spread across the slope from east to west, then downwards, downwards, uncannily swift, and all the green herbage of that wide vista was being mown as by a giant sickle, leaving only the vast moving shadow, extending, deepening, and moving rapidly nearer.

When Leiningen's men, behind their barrier of water, perceived the approach of the long-expected foe, they gave vent to their suspense in screams and imprecations. But as the distance began to lessen between the "sons of hell" and the water ditch, they relapsed into silence. Before the advance of that awe-inspiring throng, their belief in the powers of the boss began to steadily dwindle.

Even Leiningen himself, who had ridden up just in time to restore their loss of heart by a display of unshakable calm, even he could not free himself from a qualm of malaise. Yonder were thousands of millions of voracious jaws, bearing down upon him and only a suddenly insignificant, narrow ditch lay between him and his men being gnawed to the bones "before you can spit three times."

Hadn't his brain for once taken on more than it could manage? If the blighters decided to rush the ditch, fill it to the brim with their corpses, there'd still be more than enough to destroy every trace of that cranium of his. The planter's chin jutted; they hadn't got him yet, and he'd see to it they never would. While he could think at all, he'd flout both death and the devil.

The hostile army was approaching in perfect formation; no human battalions, however well drilled, could ever hope to rival the precision of that advance. Along a front that moved forward as uniformly as a straight line, the ants drew nearer and nearer to the water-ditch. Then, when they learned through their scouts the nature of the obstacle, the two outlying wings of the army detached themselves from the main body and marched down the western and eastern sides of the ditch.

This surrounding manoeuvre took rather more than an hour to accomplish; no doubt the ants expected that at some point they would find a crossing.

During this outflanking movement by the wings, the army on the centre and southern front remained still. The besieged were therefore able to contemplate at their leisure the thumb-long, reddish-black, long-legged insects; some of the Indians believed they could see, too, intent on them, the brilliant, cold eyes, and the razor-edged mandibles, of this host of infinity.

It is not easy for the average person to imagine that an animal, not to mention an insect, can *think*. But now both the European brain of Leiningen and the primitive brains of the Indians began to stir with the unpleasant forboding that inside every single one of the deluge of insects dwelt a thought. And that thought was: Ditch or no ditch, we'll get to your flesh!

Not until four o'clock did the wings reach the "horseshoe" ends of the ditch, only to find these ran into the great river. Through some kind of secret telegraphy, the report must then have flashed very swiftly indeed along the entire enemy line. And Leiningen, riding—no longer casually—along his side of the ditch, noticed by energetic and widespread movements of troops that for some unknown reason the news of the check had its greatest effect on the southern front, where the main army was massed. Perhaps the failure to find a way over the ditch was persuading the ants to withdraw from the plantation in search of spoils more easily attainable.

An immense flood of ants, about a hundred yards in width, was pouring in a glimmering-black cataract down the far slope of the ditch. Many thousands were already drowning in the sluggish, creeping flow, but they were followed by troop after troop, who clambered over their sinking comrades, and then themselves served as dying bridges to the reserves hurrying on in their rear.

Shoals of ants were being carried away by the current into the middle of the ditch, where gradually they broke asunder and then, exhausted by their struggles, vanished below the surface. Nevertheless, the wavering, floundering hundred-yard front was remorselessly if slowly advancing towards the besieged on the other bank. Leiningen had been wrong when he supposed the enemy would first have to fill the ditch with their bodies before they could cross; instead, they merely needed to act as stepping-stones, as they swam and sank, to the hordes ever pressing onwards from behind.

Near Leiningen a few mounted herdsmen awaited his orders. He sent one to the weir—the river must be damned more strongly to increase the speed and power of the water coursing through the ditch.

A second peon was dispatched to the outhouses to bring spades and petrol sprinklers. A third rode away to summon to the zone of the offensive all the men, except the observation posts, on the nearby sections of the ditch, which were not yet actively threatened.

The ants were getting across far more quickly than Leiningen would have deemed possible. Impelled by the mighty cascade behind them, they struggled nearer and nearer to the inner bank. The momentum of the attack was so great that neither the tardy flow of the stream nor its downward pull could exert its proper force; and into the gap left by every submerging insect, hastened forward a dozen more.

When reinforcements reached Leiningen, the invaders were halfway over. The planter had to admit to himself that it was only by a stroke of luck for him that the ants were attempting the crossing on a relatively short front: had they assaulted simultaneously along the entire length of the ditch, the outlook for the defenders would have been black indeed.

Even as it was, it could hardly be described as rosy, though the planter seemed quite unaware that death in a gruesome form was drawing closer and closer. As the war between his brain and the "act of God" reached its climax, the very shadow of annihilation began to pale to Leiningen, who now felt like a champion in a new Olympic game, a gigantic and thrilling contest, from which he was determined to emerge victor. Such, indeed, was his aura of confidence that the Indians forgot their stupefied fear of the peril only a yard or two away; under the planter's supervision, they began fervidly digging up to the edge of the bank and throwing clods of earth and spadefuls of sand into the midst of the hostile fleet.

The petrol sprinklers, hitherto used to detroy pests and blights on the plantation, were also brought into action. Streams of evil-reeking oil now soared and fell over an enemy already in disorder through the bombardment of earth and sand.

The ants responded to these vigorous and successful measures of defence by further developments of their offensive. Entire clumps of huddling insects began to roll down the opposite bank into the water. At the same time, Leiningen noticed that the ants were now attacking along an ever-widening front. As the numbers both of his men and his petrol sprinklers were severely limited, this rapid extension of the line of battle was becoming an overwhelming danger.

To add to his difficulties, the very clods of earth they flung into that black floating carpet often whirled fragments towards the defenders' side, and here and there dark ribbons were already mounting the inner bank. True, wherever a man saw these they could still be driven back into the water by spadefuls of earth or jets of petrol. But the file of defenders was too sparse and scattered to hold off at all points these landing parties, and though the peons toiled like madmen, their plight became momently more perilous.

One man struck with his spade at an enemy clump, did not draw it back quickly enough from the water; in a trice the wooden haft swarmed with upward scurrying insects. With a curse, he dropped the spade into the ditch; too late, they were already on his body. They lost no time; wherever they encountered bare flesh they bit deeply; a few, bigger than the rest, carried in their hindquarters a sting which injected a burning and paralyzing venom. Screaming, frantic with pain, the peon danced and twirled like a dervish.

Realizing that another such casualty, yes, perhaps this alone, might plunge his men into confusion and destroy their morale, Leiningen roared in a bellow louder than the yells of the victim: "Into the petrol, idiot! Douse your paws in the petrol!" The dervish ceased his pirouette as if transfixed, then tore off his shirt and plunged his arm and the ants hanging to it up to the shoulder in one of the large open tins of petrol. But even then the fierce mandibles did not slacken; another peon had to help him squash and detach each separate insect.

Distracted by the episode, some defenders had turned away from the ditch. And now cries of fury, a thudding of spades, and a wild trampling to and fro, showed that the ants had made full use of the interval, though luckily only a few had managed to get across. The men set to work again desperately with the barrage of earth and sand. Meanwhile an old Indian, who acts as medicine man to the plantation workers, gave the bitten peon a drink he had prepared some hours before, which, he claimed, possessed the virtue of dissolving and weakening ants' venom.

Leiningen surveyed his position. A dispassionate observer would have estimated the odds against him at a thousand to one. But then such an onlooker would have reckoned only by what he saw—the advance of myriad battalions of ants against the futile efforts of a few defenders—and not by the unseen activity that can go on in a man's brain.

For Leiningen had not erred when he decided he would fight elemental with elemental. The water in the ditch was beginning to rise; the stronger damming of the river was making itself apparent.

Visibly the swiftness and power of the masses of water increased, swirling into quicker and quicker movement its living black surface, dispersing its pattern, carrying away more and more of it on the hastening current.

Victory had been snatched from the very jaws of defeat. With a hysterical shout of joy, the peons feverishly intensified their bombardment of earth clods and sand.

And now the wide cataract down the opposite bank was thinning and ceasing, as if the ants were becoming aware that they could not attain their aim. They were scurrying back up the slope to safety.

All the troops so far hurled into the ditch had been sacrificed in vain. Drowned and floundering insects eddied in thousands along the flow, while Indians running on the bank destroyed every swimmer that reached the side.

Not until the ditch curved towards the east did the

scattered ranks assemble again in a coherent mass. And now, exhausted and half-numbed, they were in no condition to ascend the bank. Fusillades of clods drove them around the bend towards the mouth of the ditch and then into the river, wherein they vanished without leaving a trace.

The news ran swiftly along the entire chain of outposts, and soon a long scattered line of laughing men could be seen hastening along the ditch towards the scene of victory.

For once they seemed to have lost all their native reserve, for it was in wild abandon now they celebrated the triumph—as if there were no longer thousands of millions of merciless, cold and hungry eyes watching them from the opposite bank, watching and waiting.

The sun sank behind the rim of the tamarind wood and twilight deepened into night. It was not only hoped but expected that the ants would remain quiet until dawn. But to defeat any forlorn attempt at a crossing, the flow of water through the ditch was powerfully increased by opening the dam still further.

In spite of this impregnable barrier, Leiningen was not yet altogether convinced that the ants would not venture another surprise attack. He ordered his men to camp along the bank overnight. He also detailed parties of them to patrol the ditch in two of his motor cars and ceaselessly to illuminate the surface of the water with headlights and electric torches.

After having taken all the precautions he deemed necessary, the farmer ate his supper with considerable appetite and went to bed. His slumbers were in no wise disturbed by the memory of the waiting, live, twenty square miles.

Dawn found a thoroughly refreshed and active Leiningen riding along the edge of the ditch. The planter saw before him a motionless and unaltered throng of besiegers. He studied the wide belt of water between them and the plantation, and for a moment almost regretted that the fight had ended so soon and so simply. In the comforting, matter-of-fact light of morning, it seemed to him now that the ants hadn't the ghost of a chance to cross the ditch. Even if they plunged headlong into it on all three fronts at once, the force of the now powerful current would inevitably sweep them away. He had got quite a thrill out of the fight—a pity it was already over.

He rode along the eastern and southern sections of the ditch and found everything in order. He reached the western section, opposite the tamarind wood, and here, contrary to the other battle fronts, he found the enemy very busy indeed. The trunks and branches of the trees and the creepers of the lianas, on the far bank of the ditch, fairly swarmed with industrious insects. But instead of eating the leaves there and then, they were merely gnawing through the stalks, so that a thick green shower fell steadily to the ground.

No doubt they were victualling columns sent out to obtain provender for the rest of the army. The discovery did not surprise Leiningen. He did not need to be told that ants are intelligent, that certain species even use others as milch cows, watchdogs, and slaves. He was well aware of their power of adaptation, their sense of discipline, their marvelous talent for organization.

His belief that a foray to supply the army was in progress was strengthened when he saw the leaves that fell to the ground being dragged to the troops waiting outside the wood. Then all at once he realized the aim that rain of green was intended to serve.

Each single leaf, pulled or pushed by dozens of toiling insects, was borne straight to the edge of the ditch. Even as Macbeth watched the approach of Birnam Wood in the hands of his enemies, Leiningen saw the tamarind wood move nearer and nearer in the mandibles of the ants. Unlike the fey Scot, however, he did not lose his nerve; no witches had prophesied his doom, and if they had he would have slept just as soundly. All the same, he was forced to admit to himself that the situation was now far more ominous than that of the day before.

He had thought it impossible for the ants to build rafts for themselves—well, here they were, coming in thousands, more than enough to bridge the ditch. Leaves after leaves rustled down the slope into the water, where the current drew them away from the bank and carried them into midstream. And every single leaf carried several ants. This time the farmer did not trust to the alacrity of his messengers. He galloped away, leaning from his saddle and yelling orders as he rushed past outpost after outpost: "Bring petrol pumps to the southwest front! Issue spades to every man along the line facing the wood!" And arrived at the eastern and southern sections, he dispatched every man except the observation posts to the menaced west.

Then, as he rode past the stretch where the ants had failed to cross the day before, he witnessed a brief but impressive scene. Down the slope of the distant hill there came towards him a singular being, writhing rather than running, an animal-like blackened statue with a shapeless head and four quivering feet that knuckled under almost ceaselessly. When the creature reached the far bank of the ditch and collapsed opposite Leiningen, he recognized it as a pampas stag, covered over and over with ants.

It had strayed near the zone of the army. As usual, they had attacked its eyes first. Blinded, it had reeled in the madness of hideous torment straight into the ranks of its persecutors, and now the beast swayed to and fro in its death agony.

With a shot from his rifle Leiningen put it out of its misery. Then he pulled out his watch. He hadn't a second to lose, but for life itself he could not have denied his curiosity the satisfaction of knowing how long the ants would take—for personal reasons, so to speak. After six minutes the white polished bones alone remained. That's how he himself would look before you can—Leiningen spat once, and put spurs to his horse.

The sporting zest with which the excitement of the novel contest had inspired him the day before had now vanished; in its place was a cold and violent purpose. He would send these vermin back to the hell where they belonged, somehow, anyhow. Yes, but how, was indeed the question; as things stood at present it looked as if the devils would raze him and his men from the earth instead. He had underestimated the might of the enemy; he really would have to bestir himself if he hoped to outwit them.

The biggest danger now, he decided, was the point where the western section of the ditch curved southwards. And arrived there, he found his worst expectations justified. The very power of the current had huddled the leaves and their crews of ants so close together at the bend that the bridge was almost ready.

True, streams of petrol and clumps of earth still prevented a landing. But the number of floating leaves was increasing ever more swiftly. It could not be long now before a stretch of water a mile in length was decked by a green pontoon over which the ants could rush in millions.

Leiningen galloped to the weir. The damming of the river was controlled by a wheel on its bank. The planter ordered the man at the wheel first to lower the water in the ditch almost to vanishing point, next to wait a moment, then suddenly to let the river in again. This manoeuvre of lowering and raising the surface, of decreasing then increasing the flow of water through the ditch, was to be repeated over and over again until further notice.

This tactic was at first successful. The water in the ditch sank, and with it the film of leaves. The green fleet nearly reached the bed and the troops on the far bank swarmed down the slope to it. Then a violent flow of water at the original depth raced through the ditch, overwhelming leaves and ants, and sweeping them along.

This intermittent rapid flushing prevented just in time the almost completed fording of the ditch. But it also flung here and there squads of the enemy vanguard simultaneously up the inner bank. These seemed to know their duty only too well, and lost no time accomplishing it. The air rang with the curses of bitten Indians. They had removed their shirts and pants to detect the quicker the upwards-hastening insects; when they saw one, they crushed it; and fortunately the onslaught as yet was only by skirmishers.

Again and again, the water sank and rose, carrying leaves and drowned ants away with it. It lowered once more nearly to its bed; but this time the exhausted defenders waited in vain for the flush of destruction. Leiningen sensed disaster; something must have gone wrong with the machinery of the dam. Then a sweating peon tore up to him:

"They're over!"

While the besieged were concentrating upon the defense of the stretch opposite the wood, the seemingly unaffected line beyond the wood had become the theatre of decisive action. Here the defenders' front was sparse and scattered; everyone who could be spared had hurried away to the south.

Just as the man at the weir had lowered the water almost to the bed of the ditch, the ants on a wide front began another attempt at a direct crossing like that of the preceding day. Into the emptied bed poured an irresistible throng. Rushing across the ditch, they attained the inner bank before the slow-witted Indians fully grasped the situation. Their frantic screams dumbfounded the man at the weir. Before he could direct the river anew into the safeguarding bed he saw himself surrounded by raging ants. He ran like the others, ran for his life.

When Leiningen heard this, he knew the plantation was doomed. He wasted no time bemoaning the inevitable. For as long as there was the slightest chance of success, he had stood his ground, and now any further resistance was both useless and dangerous. He fired three revolver shots into the air—the prearranged signal for his men to retreat instantly within the "inner moat." Then he rode towards the ranch-house.

This was two miles from the point of invasion. There was therefore time enough to prepare the second line of defense against the advent of the ants. Of the three great petrol cisterns near the house, one had already been half emptied by the constant withdrawals needed for the pumps during the fight at the water ditch. The remaining petrol in it was now drawn off through underground pipes into the concrete trench which encircled the ranch-house and its outbuildings.

And there, drifting in twos and threes, Leiningen's men reached him. Most of them were obviously trying to preserve an air of calm and indifference, belied, however, by their restless glances and knitted brows. One could see their belief in a favorable outcome of the struggle was already considerably shaken.

The planter called his peons around him.

"Well, lads," he began, "we've lost the first round. But we'll smash the beggars yet, don't you worry. Anyone who thinks otherwise can draw his pay here and now and push off. There are rafts enough and to spare on the river and plenty of time still to reach 'em."

Not a man stirred.

Leiningen acknowledged his silent vote of confidence with a laugh that was half a grunt. "That's the stuff, lads. Too bad if you'd missed the rest of the show, eh? Well, the fun won't start till morning. Once these blighters turn tail, there'll be plenty of work for everyone and higher wages all around. And now run along and get something to eat; you've earned it all right."

In the excitement of the fight the greater part of the day had passed without the men once pausing to snatch a bite. Now that the ants were for the time being out of sight, and the "wall of petrol" gave a stronger feeling of security, hungry stomachs began to assert their claims.

The bridges over the concrete ditch were removed. Here and there solitary ants had reached the ditch; they gazed at the petrol meditatively, then scurried back again. Apparently they had little interest at the moment for what lay beyond the evil-reeking barrier; the abundant spoils of the plantation were the main attraction. Soon the trees, shrubs and beds for miles around were hulled with ants zealously gobbling the yield of long weary months of strenuous toil.

As twilight began to fall, a cordon of ants marched around the petrol trench, but as yet made no move towards its brink. Leiningen posted sentries with headlights and electric torches, then withdrew to his office, and began to reckon up his losses. He estimated these as large, but, in comparison with his bank balance, by no means unbearable. He worked out in some detail a scheme of intensive cultivation which would enable him, before very long, to more than compensate himself for the damage now being wrought to his crops. It was with a contented mind that he finally betook himself to bed where he slept deeply until dawn, undisturbed by any thought that next day little more might be left of him than a glistening skeleton.

He rose with the sun and went out on the flat roof of his house. And a scene like one from Dante lay around him; for miles in every direction there was nothing but a black, glittering multitude, a multitude of rested, sated, but none the less voracious ants: yes, look as far as one might, one could see nothing but that rustling black throng, except in the north, where the great river drew a boundary they could not hope to pass. But even the high stone breakwater, along the bank of the river, which Leiningen had built as a defense against inundations, was, like the paths, the shorn trees and shrubs, the ground itself, black with ants.

So their greed was not glutted in razing the vast plantation? Not by a long chalk; they were all the more eager now on a rich and certain booty—four hundred men, numerous horses, and bursting granaries.

At first it seemed that the petrol trench would serve its purpose. The besiegers sensed the peril of swimming it, and made no move to plunge blindly over its brink. Instead they devised a better manoeuvre; they began to collect shreds of bark, twigs and dried leaves and dropped these into the petrol. Everything green, which could have been similarly used, had long since been eaten. After a time, though, a long procession could be seen bringing from the west the tamarind leaves used as rafts the day before.

Since the petrol, unlike the water in the outer ditch, was perfectly still, the refuse stayed where it was thrown. It was several hours before the ants succeeded in covering an appreciable part of the surface. At length, however, they were ready to proceed to a direct attack.

Their storm troops swarmed down the concrete side, scrambled over the supporting surface of twigs and leaves, and impelled these over the few remaining streaks of open petrol until they reached the other side. Then they began to climb up this to make straight for the helpless garrison.

During the entire offensive, the planter sat peacefully, watching them with interest, but not stirring a muscle. Moreover, he had ordered his men not to disturb in any way whatever the advancing horde. So they squatted listlessly along the bank of the ditch and waited for a sign from the boss.

The petrol was now covered with ants. A few had climbed the inner concrete wall and were scurrying towards the defenders.

"Everyone back from the ditch!" roared Leiningen. The

men rushed away, without the slightest idea of his plan. He stooped forward and cautiously dropped into the ditch a stone which split the floating carpet and its living freight, to reveal a gleaming patch of petrol. A match spurted, sank down to the oily surface—Leiningen sprang back; in a flash a towering rampart of fire encompassed the garrison.

This spectacular and instant repulse threw the Indians into ecstasy. They applauded, yelled and stamped, like children at a pantomime. Had it not been for the awe in which they held the boss, they would infallibly have carried him shoulder high.

It was some time before the petrol burned down to the bed of the ditch, and the wall of smoke and flame began to lower. The ants had retreated in a wide circle from the devastation, and innumerable charred fragments along the outer bank showed that the flames had spread from the holocaust in the ditch well into the ranks beyond, where they had wrought havoc far and wide.

Yet the perseverence of the ants was by no means broken; indeed, each setback seemed only to whet it. The concrete cooled, the flicker of the dying flames wavered and vanished, petrol from the second tank poured into the trench—and the ants marched forward anew to the attack.

The foregoing scene repeated itself in every detail, except that on this occasion less time was needed to bridge the ditch, for the petrol was now already filmed by a layer of ash. Once again they withdrew; once again petrol flowed into the ditch. Would the creatures never learn that their self-sacrificing was utterly senseless? It really was senseless, wasn't it? Yes, of course it was senseless—provided the defenders had an *unlimited* supply of petrol.

When Leiningen reached this stage of reasoning, he felt for the first time since the arrival of the ants that his confidence was deserting him. His skin began to creep; he loosened his collar. Once the devils were over the trench there wasn't a chance in hell for him and his men. God, what a prospect, to be eaten alive like that!

For the third time the flames immolated the attacking troops, and burned down to extinction. Yet the ants were coming on again as if nothing had happened. And meanwhile Leiningen had made a discovery that chilled him to the bone—petrol was no longer flowing into the ditch. Something must be blocking the outflow pipe of the third and last cistern—a snake or a dead rat? Whatever it was, the ants could be held off no longer, unless petrol could by some method be led from the cistern into the ditch.

Then Leiningen remembered that in an outhouse nearby were two old disused fire engines. Spry as never before in their lives, the peons dragged them out of the shed, connected their pumps to the cistern, uncoiled and laid the hose. They were just in time to aim a stream of petrol at a column of ants that had already crossed and drive them back down the incline into the ditch. Once more an oily girdle surrounded the garrison, once more it was possible to hold the position—for the moment.

It was obvious, however, that this last resource meant only the postponement of defeat and death. A few of the peons fell on their knees and began to pray; others, skrieking insanely, fired their revolvers at the black, advancing masses, as if they felt their despair was pitiful enough to sway fate itself to mercy.

At length, two of the men's nerves broke: Leiningen saw a naked Indian leap over the north side of the petrol trench, quickly followed by a second. They sprinted with incredible speed towards the river. But their fleetness did not save them; long before they could attain the rafts, the enemy covered their bodies from head to foot.

In the agony of their torment, both sprang blindly into the wide river, where enemies no less sinister awaited them. Wild screams of mortal anguish informed the breathless onlookers that crocodiles and sword-toothed piranhas were no less ravenous than ants, and even nimbler in reaching their prey.

In spite of this bloody warning, more and more men showed they were making up their minds to run the blockade. Anything, even a fight midstream against alligators, seemed better than powerlessly waiting for death to come and slowly consume their living bodies.

Leiningen flogged his brain till it reeled. Was there nothing on earth could sweep this devil's spawn back into the hell from which it came?

Then out of the inferno of his bewilderment rose a terrifying inspiration. Yes, one hope remained, and one alone. It might be possible to dam the great river completely, so that its waters would fill not only the water-ditch but overflow into the entire gigantic "saucer" of land in which lay the plantation.

The far bank of the river was too high for the waters to escape that way. The stone breakwater ran between the river and the plantation; its only gaps occurred where the "horse-shoe" ends of the water-ditch passed into the river. So its waters would not only be forced to inundate into the plantation, they would also be held there by the breakwater until they rose to its own high level. In half an hour, perhaps even earlier, the plantation and its hostile army of occupation would be flooded.

The ranch-house and outbuildings stood upon rising ground. Their foundations were higher than the breakwater, so the flood would not reach them. And any remaining ants trying to ascend the slope could be repulsed by petrol.

It was possible—yes, if one could only get to the dam! A distance of nearly two miles lay between the ranch-house and the weir—two miles of ants. Those two peons had managed only a fifth of that distance at the cost of their lives. Was there an Indian daring enough after that to run the gauntlet five times as far? Hardly likely; and if there were, his prospect of getting back was almost nil.

No, there was only one thing for it, he'd have to make the attempt himself; he might just as well be running as sitting still, anyway, when the ants finally got him. Besides, there *was* a bit of a chance. Perhaps the ants weren't so almighty, after all; perhaps he had allowed the mass suggestion of that evil black throng to hypnotize him, just as a snake fascinates and overpowers.

The ants were building their bridges. Leiningen got up on a chair. "Hey, lads, listen to me!" he cried. Slowly and listlessly, from all sides of the trench, the men began to shuffle towards him, the apathy of death already stamped on their faces.

"Listen, lads!" he shouted. "You're frightened of those beggars, but you're a damn sight more frightened of me, and I'm proud of you. There's still a chance to save our lives—by flooding the plantation from the river. Now one of you might manage to get as far as the weir—but he'd never come back. Well, I'm not going to let you try it; if I did I'd be worse than one of those ants. No, I called the tune, and now I'm going to pay the piper.

"The moment I'm over the ditch, set fire to the petrol. That'll allow time for the flood to do the trick. Then all you have to do is to wait here all snug and quiet till I'm back. Yes, I'm coming back, trust me"—he grinned—"when I've finished my slimming cure."

He pulled on high leather boots, drew heavy gauntlets over his hand, and stuffed the space betwen breeches and boots, gauntlets and arms, shirt and neck, with rags soaked in petrol. With close-fitting mosquito goggles he shielded his eyes, knowing too well the ants' dodge of first robbing their victim of sight. Finally, he plugged his nostrils and ears with cotton-wool, and let the peons drench his clothes with petrol.

He was about to set off when the old Indian medicine man came up to him; he had a wondrous salve, he said, prepared from a species of chafer whose odor was intolerable to ants. Yes, this odor protected these chafers from the attacks of even the most murderous ants. The Indian smeared the boss's boots, his gauntlets, and his face over and over with the extract.

Leiningen then remembered the paralyzing effect of ants' venom, and the Indian gave him a gourd full of the medicine he had administered to the bitten peon at the water-ditch. The planter drank it down without noticing its bitter taste; his mind was already at the weir.

He started off towards the northwest corner of the trench. With a bound he was over—and among the ants.

The beleaguered garrison had no opportunity to watch Leiningen's race against death. The ants were climbing the inner bank again—the lurid ring of petrol blazed aloft. For the fourth time that day the reflection from the fire shone on the sweating faces of the imprisoned men, and on the reddish-black cuirasses of their oppressors. The red and blue, dark-edged flames leaped vividly now, celebrating what? The funeral pyre of the four hundred, or of the hosts of destruction?

Leiningen ran. He ran in long, equal strides, with only one thought, one sensation, in his being—he *must* get through. He dodged all trees and shrubs; except for the split seconds his soles touched the ground the ants should have no opportunity to alight on him. That they would get to him soon, despite the salve on his boots, the petrol on his clothes, he realized only too well, but he knew even more surely that he must, and that he would, get to the weir.

Apparently the salve was of some use after all; not until he had reached halfway did he feel ants under his clothes, and a few on his face. Mechanically, in his stride, he struck at them, scarcely conscious of their bites. He saw he was drawing

appreciably nearer the weir—the distance grew less and less—
sank to five hundred—three—two—one hundred yards.

Then he was at the weir and gripping the ant-hulled wheel.
Hardly had he seized it when a horde of infuriated ants flowed
over his hands, arms and shoulders. He started the wheel—
before it turned once on its axis the swarm covered his face.
Leiningen strained like a madman, his lips pressed tight; if he
opened them to draw breath ...

He turned and turned; slowly the dam lowered until it
reached the bed of the river. Already the water was overflowing
the ditch. Another minute, and the river was pouring through
the nearby gap in the breakwater. The flooding of the
plantation had begun.

Leiningen let go the wheel. Now, for the first time, he
realized he was coated from head to foot with a layer of ants. In
spite of the petrol, his clothes were full of them, several had got
to his body or were clinging to his face. Now that he had
completed his task, he felt the smart raging over his flesh from
the bites of sawing and piercing insects.

Frantic with pain, he almost plunged into the river. To be
ripped and slashed to shreds by piranhas? Already he was
running the return journey, knocking ants from his gloves and
jacket, brushing them from his bloodied face, squashing them
to death under his clothes.

One of the creatures bit him just below the rim of his
goggles; he managed to tear it away, but the agony of the bite
and its etching acid drilled into the eye nerves; he saw now
through circles of fire into a milky mist, then he ran for a time
almost blinded, knowing that if he once tripped and fell. ...
The old Indian's brew didn't seem much good; it weakened the
poison a bit, but didn't get rid of it. His heart pounded as if it
would burst; blood roared in his ears; a giant's fist battered his
lungs.

Then he could see again, but the burning girdle of petrol

appeared infinitely far away; he could not last half that distance. Swift-changing pictures flashed through his head, episodes in his life, while in another part of his brain a cool and impartial onlooker informed this ant-blurred, gasping, exhausted bundle named Leiningen that such a rushing panorama of scenes from one's past is seen only in the moment before death.

A stone in the path . . . too weak to avoid it . . . the planter stumbled and collapsed. He tried to rise . . . he must be pinned under a rock . . . it was impossible . . . the slightest movement was impossible.

Then all at once he saw, starkly clear and huge, and, right before his eyes, furred with ants, towering and swaying in its death agony, the pampas stag. In six minutes—gnawed to the bones. God, he *couldn't* die like that! And something outside him seemed to drag him to his feet. He tottered. He began to stagger forward again.

Through the blazing ring hurtled an apparition which, as soon as it reached the ground on the inner side, fell full length and did not move. Leiningen, at the moment he made that leap through the flames, lost consciousness for the first time in his life. As he lay there, with glazing eyes and lacerated face, he appeared a man returned from the grave. The peons rushed to him, stripped off his clothes, tore away the ants from a body that seemed almost one open wound; in some places the bones were showing. They carried him into the ranch-house.

As the curtain of flames lowered, one could see, in place of the illimitable host of ants, an extensive vista of water. The thwarted river had swept over the plantation, carrying with it the entire army. The water had collected and mounted in the great "saucer," while the ants had in vain attempted to reach the hill on which stood the ranch-house. The girdle of flames held them back.

And so, imprisoned between water and fire, they had been delivered into the annihilation that was their god. And near the farther mouth of the water-ditch, where the stone mole had its second gap, the ocean swept the lost battalions into the river to vanish forever.

The ring of fire dwindled as the water mounted to the petrol trench, and quenched the dimming flames. The inundation rose higher and higher: because its outflow was impeded by the timber and underbrush it had carried along with it, its surface required some time to reach the top of the high stone breakwater and discharge over it the rest of the shattered army.

It swelled over ant-stippled shrubs and bushes, until it washed against the foot of the knoll whereon the besieged had taken refuge. For a while an alluvium of ants tried again and again to attain this dry land, only to be repulsed by streams of petrol back into the merciless flood.

Leiningen lay on his bed, his body swathed from head to foot in bandages. With fomentations and salves, they had managed to stop the bleeding, and had dressed his many wounds. Now they thronged around him, one question in every face. Would he recover? "He won't die," said the old man who had bandaged him, "if he doesn't want to."

The planter opened his eyes. "Everything in order?" he asked.

"They're gone," said his nurse. "To hell." He held out to his master a gourd full of a powerful sleeping-draught. Leiningen gulped it down.

"I told you I'd come back," he murmured, "even if I am a bit streamlined." He grinned and shut his eyes. He slept.

THE MAN WHO SOLD ROPE TO THE GNOLES

IDRIS SEABRIGHT

The gnoles had a bad reputation, and Mortensen was quite aware of this. But he reasoned, correctly enough, that cordage must be something for which the gnoles had a long unsatisfied want, and he saw no reason why he should not be the one to sell it to them. What a triumph such a sale would be! The district sales manager might single out Mortensen for special mention at the annual sales-force dinner. It would help his sales quota enormously. And, after all, it was none of his business what the gnoles used cordage for.

Mortensen decided to call on the gnoles on Thursday morning. On Wednesday night he went through his *Manual of Modern Salesmanship,* underscoring things.

"The mental states through which the mind passes in making a purchase," he read, "have been catalogued as: 1) arousal of interest 2) increase of knowledge 3) adjustment to needs. . . ." There were seven mental states listed, and Mortensen underscored all of them. Then he went back and double-scored No. 1, arousal of interest, No. 4, appreciation of suitability, and No. 7, decision to purchase. He turned the page.

"Two qualities are of exceptional importance to a salesman," he read. "They are adaptability and knowledge of merchandise." Mortensen underlined the qualities. "Other highly desirable attributes are physical fitness, a high ethical standard, charm of manner, a dogged persistence, and unfailing courtesy." Mortensen underlined these too. But he read on to the end of the paragraph without underscoring anything more, and it may be that his failure to put "tact and keen power of observation" on a footing with the other attributes of a salesman was responsible for what happened to him.

The gnoles live on the very edge of Terra Cognita, on the far side of a wood which all authorities unite in describing as dubious. Their house is narrow and high, in architecture a blend of Victorian Gothic and Swiss chalet. Though the house needs paint, it is kept in good repair. Thither on Thursday morning, sample case in hand, Mortensen took his way.

No path leads to the house of the gnoles, and it is always dark in that dubious wood. But Mortensen, remembering what he had learned at his mother's knee concerning the odor of gnoles, found the house quite easily. For a moment he stood hesitating before it. His lips moved as he repeated, "Good morning, I have come to supply your cordage requirements," to himself. The words were the beginning of his sales talk. Then he went up and rapped on the door.

The gnoles were watching him through holes they had bored in the trunks of trees; it is an artful custom of theirs to which the prime authority on gnoles attests. Mortensen's knock almost threw them into confusion; it was so long since anyone had knocked at their door. Then the senior gnole, the one who never leaves the house, went flitting up from the cellars and opened it.

The senior gnole is a little like a Jerusalem artichoke made of India rubber, and he has small red eyes which are faceted in the same way that gemstones are. Mortensen had been expecting something unusual, and when the gnole opened the door he bowed politely, took off his hat, and smiled. He had got past the sentence about cordage requirements and into an enumeration of the different types of cordage his firm manufactured when the gnole, by turning his head to the side, showed him that he had no ears. Nor was there anything on his head which could take their place in the conduction of sound. Then the gnole opened his little fanged mouth and let Mortensen look at his narrow, ribbony tongue. As a tongue it was no more fit for human speech than was a serpent's. Judging from his appearance, the gnole could not safely be assigned to any of the four physio-characterological types mentioned in the *Manual;* and for the first time Mortensen felt a definite qualm.

Nonetheless, he followed the gnole unhesitatingly when the creature motioned him within. Adaptability, he told himself, adaptability must be his watchword. Enough adaptability, and his knees might even lose their tendency to shakiness.

It was the parlor the gnole led him to. Mortensen's eyes widened as he looked around it. There were whatnots in the corners, and cabinets of curiosities, and on the fretwork table an album with gilded hasps; who knows whose pictures were in it? All around the walls in brackets, where in lesser houses the people display ornamental plates, were emeralds as big as your head. The gnoles set great store by their emeralds. All the light in the dim room came from them.

Mortensen went through the phrases of his sales talk mentally. It distressed him that that was the only way he could go through them. Still, adaptability! The gnole's interest was already aroused, or he would never have asked Mortensen into the parlor; and as soon as the gnole saw the various cordages the sample case contained he would no doubt proceed of his own accord through "appreciation of suitability" to "desire to possess."

Mortensen sat down in the chair the gnole indicated and opened his sample case. He got out henequen cable-laid rope, an assortment of ply and yarn goods, and some superlative slender abaca fiber rope. He even showed the gnole a few soft yarns and twines made of cotton and jute.

On the back of an envelope he wrote prices for hanks and cheeses of the twines, and for fifty- and hundred-foot lengths of the ropes. Laboriously he added details about the strength, durability, and resistance to climatic conditions of each sort of cord. The senior gnole watched him intently, putting his little feet on the top rung of his chair and poking at the facets of his left eye now and then with a tentacle. In the cellars from time to time someone would scream.

Mortensen began to demonstrate his wares. He showed the gnole the slip and resilience of one rope, the tenacity and stubborn strength of another. He cut a tarred hemp rope in two and laid a five-foot piece on the parlor floor to show the gnole how absolutely "neutral" it was, with no tendency to untwist of its own accord. He even showed the gnole how nicely some of the cotton twines made up in square knotwork.

They settled at last on two ropes of abaca fiber, 3/16 and 5/8 inch in diameter. The gnole wanted an enormous quantity. Mortensen's comment on those ropes, "unlimited strength and durability," seemed to have attracted him.

Soberly Mortensen wrote the particulars down in his order book, but ambition was setting his brain on fire. The gnoles, it seemed, would be regular customers; and after the gnoles, why should he not try the Gibbelins? They too must have a need for rope.

Mortensen closed his order book. On the back of the same

envelope he wrote, for the gnole to see, that delivery would be made within ten days. Terms were 30 per cent with order, balance upon receipt of goods.

The senior gnole hesitated. Shyly he looked at Mortensen with his little red eyes. Then he got down the smallest of the emeralds from the wall and handed it to him.

The sales representative stood weighing it in his hands. It was the smallest of the gnoles' emeralds, but it was as clear as water, as green as grass. In the outside world it would have ransomed a Rockefeller or a whole family of Guggenheims; a legitimate profit from a transaction was one thing, but this was another; "a high ethical standard"—any kind of ethical standard—would forbid Mortensen to keep it. He weighed it a moment longer. Then with a deep, deep sigh he gave the emerald back.

He cast a glance around the room to see if he could find something which would be more negotiable. And in an evil moment he fixed on the senior gnole's auxiliary eyes.

The senior gnole keeps his extra pair of optics on the third shelf of the curiosity cabinet with the glass doors. They look like fine dark emeralds about the size of the end of your thumb. And if the gnoles in general set store by their gems, it is nothing at all compared to the senior gnole's emotions about his extra eyes. The concern good Christian folk should feel for their soul's welfare is a shadow, a figment, a nothing, compared to what the thoroughly heathen gnole feels for those eyes. He would rather, I think, choose to be a mere miserable human being than that some vandal should lay hands on them.

If Mortensen had not been elated by his success to the point of anaesthesia, he would have seen the gnole stiffen, he would have heard him hiss, when he went over to the cabinet. All innocent, Mortensen opened the glass door, took the twin eyes out, and juggled them sacrilegiously in his hand; the gnole could feel them clink. Smiling to evince the charm of manner advised in the *Manual,* and raising his brows as one who says, "Thank you, these will do nicely," Mortensen dropped the eyes into his pocket.

The gnole growled.

The growl awoke Mortensen from his trance of euphoria. It was a growl whose meaning no one could mistake. This was clearly no time to be doggedly persistent. Mortensen made a break for the door.

The senior gnole was there before him, his network of tentacles outstretched. He caught Mortensen in them easily and wound them, flat as bandages, around his ankles and his hands. The best abaca fiber is no stronger than those tentacles; though the gnoles would find rope a convenience, they get along very well without it. Would you, dear reader, go naked if zippers should cease to be made? Growling indignantly, the gnole fished his ravished eyes from Mortensen's pockets, and then carried him down to the cellar to the fattening pens.

But great are the virtues of legitimate commerce. Though they fattened Mortensen sedulously, and, later, roasted and sauced him and ate him with real appetite, the gnoles slaughtered him in quite a humane manner and never once thought of torturing him. That is unusual, for gnoles. And they ornamented the plank on which they served him with a beautiful border of fancy knotwork made of cotton cord from his own sample case.

ABOUT THE EDITOR

Helen Hoke has had printer's ink in her blood ever since she was born in a small town in Pennsylvania. Her father owned and edited a newspaper, and she was his eager apprentice. She later became a teacher and a bookseller, and initiated the children's book departments of several distinguished American publishers. Helen Hoke now lives in New York City, having traveled extensively during a successful career in publishing. Well known for her sparkling joke books and spine-chilling anthologies, she is—not surprisingly—an avid reader, particularly of short stories.